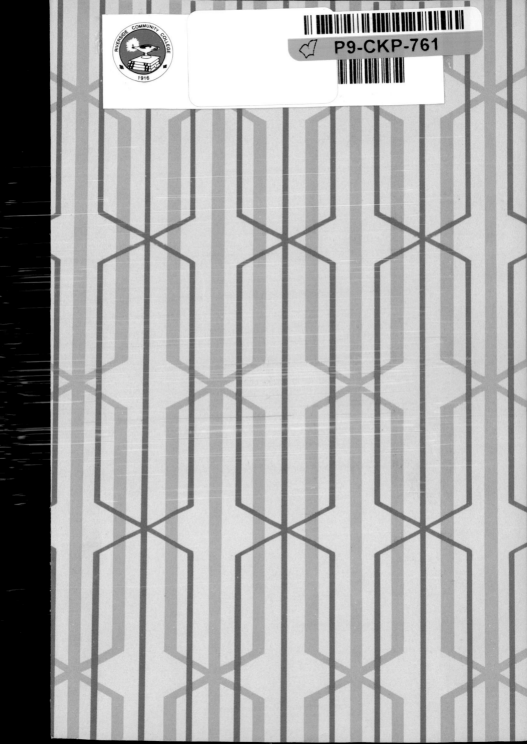

GOLDEN PHŒNIX

"Wait!" said a voice that seemed to come out of the ceiling of the
temple room.

GOLDEN PHOENIX

by

PRINCESS DER LING

Illustrated by
BERTHA LUM

Short Story Index Reprint Series

BOOKS FOR LIBRARIES PRESS
FREEPORT, NEW YORK

First Published 1932
Reprinted 1969

STANDARD BOOK NUMBER:

8369-3187-4

LIBRARY OF CONGRESS CATALOG CARD NUMBER:

70-101799

MANUFACTURED
BY
HALLMARK LITHOGRAPHERS, INC.
IN THE U.S.A.

CONTENTS

ILLUSTRATIONS

GOLDEN PHŒNIX

GOLDEN PHŒNIX

VER the old Forbidden City, in the heart of Peking, rose the monotonous beating of the solemn drums, slow, measured beating as the drums informed the populace that the Emperor had ascended the Dragon Throne on High.

"His Majesty is dead!" the people whispered. "Ming Te will reign in his stead, according to the ancient laws! His Majesty is dead! Long live His Majesty, the new Emperor!"

Within the sacred confines of the Forbidden City the eunuchs walked with solemn tread across the aged cobblestones. Their heads were bowed in sorrow. From the royal kitchens came only silence, for the court was fasting. From the quarters of the court attendants came no chattering murmur of serving maids. The solemn hush held sway over all—for all China knew, from the first drumbeat, that His Majesty was dead, and that, within the death chamber, garbed in his robes of state, the dead ruler rested on his bier, with flickering candles about him to light his way into the Hereafter.

There remained only the last sad rite of burial—and the coronation, which would make Ming Te, only nine-

3

teen years of age, ruler of China's millions, as his father had been ruler before him for half a century.

When the day of burial had been decided upon, after careful consultation of the books of signs and portents, the funeral cortege—gorgeous, solemn, and somehow terrible—wended its way out of the Forbidden City along the road strewn with yellow sand which, spread by reverent hands of loyal subjects, formed a golden pathway to the imperial tombs of Tung Ling.

There remained, then, only the coronation of Ming Te.

At least, so thought Ming Te, himself. But he was a young man who had paid slight attention to court intrigues, or the sometimes strange behavior of court officials who sought to rule China from behind the throne. Ming Te had scarcely returned from bidding sad farewell to his father when the ministers crowded about him—and kowtowed, though Ming Te had not yet been crowned.

"Your Majesty," said the Grand Councilor, "will become ruler absolute of his country. But it is not good for an Emperor to rule alone. Nor is it good for a man to fail in providing his Dynasty with an heir. Your Majesty must marry—at once!"

Ming Te was startled. He had not cared for women. There were many women at court, but Ming Te was

4

interested in none of them. To the young Emperor, women were merely symbols of trouble—for men. So he temporized.

"I am only nineteen," he stated. "There is no necessity of taking a wife so soon. There should yet be many years of life ahead of me in which to make a choice. I do not wish a wife chosen for me. I wish to choose her myself, and she must be someone who is pleasing to me!"

"Your Majesty," insisted the Grand Councilor obstinately, "would be failing in his duty to his people if he neglected to give them an Empress who would give His Majesty an heir to rule after him—and to pay homage at His Majesty's grave when he passes! It is a matter of the gravest importance!"

"But I have seen all the ladies of the court, and I am pleased with none of them!" replied Ming Te impatiently. "I know that certain things are required of the ruler, but I like not this unseemly haste."

"Your Majesty must realize that the people themselves, who look to Your Majesty for guidance, will expect him to take an Empress and to provide an heir. It is the custom. Surely, among Your Majesty's many officials of sufficient rank to provide a daughter to be Empress, there is one who pleases you!"

"I have marked them all, and there is none. However, we must show my people that their Emperor adheres to sacred custom. I shall give a garden party in honor of my coronation. I shall issue a decree commanding all daughters of officials of the first rank to attend my garden party. Perhaps there be one among them whom I have overlooked."

The garden party was planned for the next day following the coronation. The coronation took place at midnight.

It was a most momentous occasion. It signified, more than anything, that the father of Ming Te was gone forever and that his son ruled in his stead. In the palace of the coronation the candles of many colors flickered oddly and wrought strange shadows on the carved walls. Great, yellow dragons writhed about the gigantic pillars, breathing flames from flaring nostrils. On the floor before the throne the nobles of the court knelt on red satin cushions to perform the kowtows decreed by custom. Nine kowtows to the gods of heaven, of the earth, and to the Son of Heaven, Ming Te. Then the highest official in the land placed the Imperial Hat on the head of Ming Te, and he was Emperor of the Middle Kingdom.

For many moments he sat there, gazing down upon the bowed heads and kneeling figures of his officials, through whom he issued mandates to the people. Men

6

of families which had been noble from time immemorial kowtowed there before the young Ming Te. The candles guttered and sputtered, and vague whispers seemed to travel back and forth among the shadows in the corners, and under the dome of the palace which had witnessed so many coronations.

Ming Te's arms rested on the arms of his throne. The great dragon embroidered on the breast of His Majesty's robe seemed almost alive. The golden robe itself seemed to fill the dim palace of coronation with a light all its own. His thumb-ring of purest jade was like a lotus leaf, fragile and delicate, against the pallor of His Majesty's hands. The Imperial Hat of the coronation, set with many precious stones, sent out little lancets of light—as the candles flickered and sputtered and the wax dripped audibly to the tiles of the palace floor.

For many minutes His Majesty gazed at the bowed heads and kneeling figures of his officials. Then, with imperial dignity which sat upon him as naturally as though he had already ruled for a decade, he bade his officials rise.

"We wish to retire," he told them, "and rest against the fatigue of tomorrow's garden party."

The officials, departing, conversed delightedly among themselves. When His Majesty had been crowned, there had been some among them who believed that

His Majesty would decide, after all, against the garden party and thus delay the selection of an Empress. But His Majesty was keeping his promise to his advisors, and it augured well for the future.

His Majesty was calm and dignified next day, when the young maidens, daughters of officials of the first rank, began to arrive at the gates of the Forbidden City in obedience to the Imperial Decree. They guessed, many of them, the reason why His Majesty desired their presence, and there were many maiden hearts which beat faster as maiden minds peered into the future. Ming Te was young and handsome and should rule for many years. The maiden chosen to be his Empress would be fortunate indeed. So all the maidens bidden to attend came dressed in their finest raiment and wearing their manners of ceremony. Fragile, some, as lilies or lotus buds, but some were fat, and some were homely, and His Majesty noted them one by one—as they were bidden by attendants to walk and bow before the throne in the Hall of Audience—and shook his head. Secretly he was pleased. His Majesty was not ready to take a wife.

How gaily colored was the garden party! The thousands of eunuchs—some fat, some tall, some large and some small—were dressed in gorgeous robes only less elaborate than the robe of His Majesty. They were

8

stern and dignified, those eunuchs, as befitted servants of the court. The officials, too, were garbed until their glories dimmed the glory of the sun, which seemed to smile a benediction upon the fateful gathering. The yellow-tile roofs of the many palaces were like the sun itself, hotly reflecting its warm, caressing rays. The cobblestones of the many courtyards echoed to the foot-falls of eunuchs and serving maids, ladies of the court and high-ranking visitors. The question in every mind was the same:

"Will His Majesty find a maiden who pleases him?"

The officials waited hopefully. One of the last to come, though all arrived before the time stipulated in the Imperial Decree, was Golden Phœnix, daughter of a high official named Ma Su. His Majesty noted at once a coldness that descended upon the garden party with the arrival of Golden Phœnix, and wondered greatly. At last, after vainly waiting for Golden Phœnix to approach the throne, Ming Te beckoned his Grand Councilor.

"Who," asked Ming Te, "is the maiden in the robe of the hundred butterflies, and why have I not seen her before?"

The Grand Councilor was distressed, a fact that immediately aroused the curiosity of His Majesty. He pressed his question, demanding an answer.

"Her name, Your Majesty," replied the Grand Councilor at last, "is Golden Phœnix, and she is daughter of Ma Su, the firebrand. Ma Su was out of favor with Your Majesty's Imperial Father, and his daughter was not asked to court."

"She pleases me," said Ming Te simply.

This but added to the distress of the Grand Councilor.

"But she is daughter of Ma Su, whom the Board of Punishment has recommended to the Throne for discipline!"

"She pleases me," repeated His Majesty Ming Te.

"How could she please Your Majesty?" insisted the Grand Councilor. "There is little doubt that her father is a venomous traitor to the Throne. If he is given the slightest opportunity, he will be as disloyal to Your Majesty as he was suspected of being to Your Majesty's Imperial Parent."

"It is no fault of Golden Phœnix that her father is suspect," said Ming Te, "and no charges have been proved against him."

"They will most certainly be proved, Your Majesty," said the Grand Councilor vehemently. "The passing of judgment on Ma Su will be one of the first and most important matters awaiting Your Majesty's august attention!"

GOLDEN PHŒNIX

"Send the maiden to me. I wish to speak with her."

The Grand Councilor went, with vast reluctance, to bid Golden Phœnix attend upon His Majesty.

Silence fell in the Hall of Audience. Officials looked at one another in consternation. The maidens looked at one another questioningly—and at Golden Phœnix with ill-concealed resentment. Every person present in the Audience Hall knew at once that Golden Phœnix was the most beautiful maiden in the gathering. She walked proudly, as became a great lady. Her manners were gentle, and she swayed gracefully as she walked toward the throne where His Majesty sat. The Chief Eunuch hurried forward with a golden cushion upon which she might kneel to kowtow to her sovereign. Ming Te studied the maiden of the robe of a hundred butterflies—on a field of lotus green—and there was pleased approval in his glance.

Her well-deep eyes, under lashes which rose and fell softly like the wings of a gorgeous black moth, met those of His Majesty unafraid. He seemed not to notice the strained silence that held sway in the Hall of Audience, in which the light footfalls of Golden Phœnix were audible and the words which passed between Golden Phœnix and His Majesty must be heard by all.

Golden Phœnix knelt on the cushion, like a lily bending and swaying in a gentle breeze, and bowed her head to perform the kowtows decreed by custom. And the officials, horrified, scarcely believed their ears as Ming Te spoke softly.

"Lift up your head, Golden Phœnix," he commanded. "It is a custom for subjects to kowtow to their sovereign, but I wish to look into your face as we speak. Rise, then, and face me!"

Calmly Golden Phœnix rose to her feet. His Majesty asked her a few questions. He asked about matters which only those who knew their Chinese ancient Classics might answer, and Golden Phœnix answered his every question without hesitation and correctly. After a while, smiling, His Majesty bade Golden Phœnix return to her place.

When the garden party was ended at last, Ming Te called his Grand Councilor.

"The maiden Golden Phœnix finds favor in my eyes," he said simply. "It is decreed that she come to court to become my Empress!"

"Has Your Majesty forgotten that Ma Su, father of Golden Phœnix, is an evil old one, suspected already of plotting against Your Majesty in order to make himself Emperor?"

"I have forgotten nothing. But my people are happy, and there is peace in the land. I shall keep my people happy. There is no danger for me, and if any should arise I shall be strong enough in the hearts of my people to save myself, and the throne. It is my wish to wed with Golden Phœnix. Perhaps she has sufficient influence with the honorable Ma Su to change his views, so that he becomes an open friend of the Throne instead of a secret enemy. There is nothing more to be said. The words I have spoken are law!"

All the nobles, being informed, bowed to the Imperial Decree—and Golden Phœnix, loveliest of all the maidens, became Empress.

The court wedding was one of the most magnificent known to history, for Ming Te knew that he loved Golden Phœnix, that he had loved her since first he had singled her out from among all the others. Love had been kindled in the heart of Ming Te when, at the fateful garden party, his eyes had looked deeply into the eyes of Golden Phœnix. And she confessed shyly, after the ceremony, that she, too, had loved Ming Te from the beginning.

"But I am afraid," she also told him. "My father has an evil reputation. There is nothing I can do to dissuade him from his cruel ways. I am afraid that I, his daughter, shall cause you endless trouble."

"What does trouble matter, when we love each other with such a love as two people never before have known?" replied Ming Te. "We shall meet trouble, when it comes, together—together until the end of our days, which can be nothing, ever, but happy beyond words to express!"

The union of Ming Te, the handsome young Emperor, and Golden Phœnix, the intellectual and beautiful, was an idyl of love. They lived for each other. Ming Te, though Emperor, listened raptly to the advice of Golden Phœnix. Their worship was mutual, and their love story was one that caused lovers' hearts to beat faster with soft sympathy all over the Middle Kingdom.

But . . .

Even though his daughter was Empress, Ma Su was not satisfied. He wished himself to become Emperor. Now that his daughter was Empress, he could make his plans and build his plots more boldly—for His Majesty would not lightly destroy the father of the woman he loved as he loved nothing else, even the memory of his Imperial Parent. Moreover Ma Su knew the dynastic law: if a man was proved traitor to the Throne, he was decapitated at once, and all his family with him! For it had been the law forever that it was not proper to destroy the tiger and spare the cubs. If Ming Te destroyed Ma Su for treason, then, according to the old laws, he must destroy his own Empress whom he worshiped.

And when the word fled the length and breadth of China that a child had been born to Golden Phœnix Ma Su was thrice pleased. It was a great event—the birth of an Imperial Heir always was. Golden Phœnix had been fortunate above all women. She had borne Ming Te a son!

While all the country was aroused over this, gleeful and singing, Ma Su performed his master stroke. He mustered malcontents under the banner of red revolution, and, within a week of the birth of the Heir, the people were slaying and being slain in one of the most dreadful civil wars China had ever known.

The Grand Councilor and the Ministers sought audience with Ming Te. Again the Grand Councilor acted as spokesman for the kneeling officials.

"Your Majesty!" he cried. "Ma Su has at last proved himself a traitor. China is steeped in bloodshed. The people cry out against civil war. The people blame Her Majesty, the Empress. They believe that she has influenced her father against Your Majesty for some reason of her own—perhaps so that her son, if Your Majesty is forced to relinquish his throne, may become Emperor, and herself regent until he is of an age to rule! And from behind Her Majesty's regency Her Majesty's father will rule China. He will be almost

Emperor. Who knows, Your Majesty? Perhaps he may even destroy Your Majesty's son to make himself ruler in very fact!"

"What are my people's demands?" said Ming Te softly.

"They demand that Ma Su be sent into exile, or be decapitated, and that Her Majesty be ordered to commit suicide! They know the ancient law, that the root must be destroyed with the branch, the tiger cub with the tiger. Ma Su must be destroyed, and Her Majesty is his daughter! If both die, then China will have peace again, and the blood of her people no longer flow in a monstrous civil war."

Ming Te was grave as he pondered the matter for a moment.

"If I believed that the people desired Ma Su as their Emperor, I would gladly abdicate and go myself into exile—with Golden Phœnix, who is more in my heart than all my people, my throne, my own life—because she is my life!"

"Your Majesty is the divine ruler by direct descent. Your Majesty is China's rightful sovereign, and the people will not let you go. But if Your Majesty does not act against Ma Su and his daughter, then the people will storm the palace and slay Her Majesty, or force her to commit suicide."

"Would my people slay me? I should permit harm to come to Golden Phœnix only in the event of my death!"

"The people slay Your Majesty?" said the Grand Councilor in a voice vibrant with horror. "Who does not know the penalty for raising violent hands against the sovereign? Who so raises hands against Your Majesty will die himself by violence, and suffer for ninety and nine years of unbelievable torment!"

"What would you have me do?"

"We have spoken already with the voice of the people. Banish Ma Su forever or order his decapitation, and order Golden Phœnix to commit suicide!"

"I must have time to decide," said Ming Te softly; but deep in his heart he knew he could never part from Golden Phœnix of the golden heart.

Deeply troubled, he discussed the matter with Golden Phœnix. She smiled at his perplexity. Her soft palms touched his cheeks with the light caress of love.

"China is greater than our love, O Ming Te," she told him. "You must hearken to the voice of the people. I am not afraid. I shall commit suicide so that our people's wrath be appeased."

"I will never permit you," groaned Ming Te. "Rather will I doff my robes of power, go forth from my palaces and my beloved country, into exile with you—even in rags!—than be separated from you!"

17

"But the people will not let you go! And if you go, my father, whom I know to be an evil man, will rule— and his rule will be a catastrophe for our country. It is simple then. Order me to commit suicide, and I will obey. We shall be separated for only a little while— when you mount the Dragon Throne on High, we shall be together, for in death none may ever part us again!"

"I know not what comes afterward," groaned Ming Te, "nor that there is truly no separation in death. Suppose, my beloved, that death were the end, and that, once separated by the grave, we must remain forever separated? Our spirits would journey for eternity up and down the earth and never find peace—because we could not find each other! I must have time to make a decision."

Next day he called in his Grand Councilor and his Ministers and addressed them.

"I have discussed this grave matter with Her Majesty. She is not afraid to die. She places China's happiness above her own life. She will die by her own hand if I bid her. Tell my people that, so that they shall know the greatness of Golden Phœnix! But I myself cannot at once decide. I wish ten days in which to meditate. To appease the people, Her Majesty will be given into your hands to be imprisoned. At the end of ten days

I shall issue a decree of judgment."

A truce was declared when the word went forth, and for ten days the great civil war tarried. The people praised the greatness of Golden Phœnix, but did not relent toward her. She would become a saint if she committed suicide for their sake, and throughout the Empire monuments would be erected in her honor, and she would be worshiped and mourned forever by her people.

But still she must die. In that the people were adamant. Her greatness turned even the hearts of Ma Su's followers partially against him. If Golden Phœnix sacrificed herself for her Empire, Ma Su's followers themselves might rise against him to destroy him. So Ma Su, having overreached himself, waited in fear and trembling for those ten days to pass.

Golden Phœnix went to prison within the Forbidden City, where she could be watched and guarded. Her son, the Imperial Heir, was given into the hands of serving maids and court ladies to be reared.

For two days His Majesty mourned Golden Phœnix as though she were already dead; but he knew she was not and that he could not live without her. Then late in the night he garbed himself as a commoner, and like an ordinary felon followed the shadowy aisles of the Forbidden City until he arrived at the prison house of his beloved. His heart smote him as he noted the iron bars across the windows. Within that dark and dreary place slept his Empress, garbed in rough garments, fed through the bars like any common prisoner.

His Majesty's tears were flowing as he stepped close to the bars and gently spoke his beloved's name.

"Golden Phœnix! My precious Golden Phœnix! Can you hear me, beloved?"

A sound of someone stirring, and Golden Phœnix came to the window—just as the moon came out from behind the clouds and peered down upon the Forbidden City.

How changed was Golden Phœnix, even after but two days of absence! Her hair was uncovered, all the black, rich loveliness of it, and hung about her pale face like a shroud. But her eyes were glowing in the moonlight, and her slim hands came through the bars to caress the cheeks of Ming Te with their soft and gentle palms.

His Majesty knew that Golden Phœnix was garbed in ragged blue cloth such as coolie women wore, yet she hid it from her beloved. He knew that her food, rough rice, was thrust to her through the bars as though she had been a murderer; that she ate it with chopsticks of rough wood, when she had been accustomed to chopsticks of jade; that she ate from wooden bowls when she had always had plates and bowls of jade and gold. But of all these things she said nothing. Her only words of greeting were:

"I love you, Ming Te!"

His tears fell softly, and in the darkness, unseen by Ming Te, fell also the tears of Golden Phœnix. But she seemed to be happy for his sake.

"I am not afraid," she told him. "It is for our country's sake. Have you arrived at a decision?"

"No, my beloved, save this: I cannot give you up! Every way I turn, seeking some solution, I am confounded. Ma Su must be destroyed. His family must be destroyed with him. It is the old dynastic law from which there is no escape—as binding upon me as upon my people!"

"Then it is simple, Ming Te," replied Golden Phœnix. "Have courage—and faith. We shall be separated for only a little while!"

So for a long time they stood there, clasping hands through the bars of the window, mingling their tears—while the compassionate moon looked down.

"I ask but one thing, my beloved," whispered Ming Te at last, "that you do not destroy yourself without orders to spare me the necessity of rendering judgment!"

"I am my master's slave," said Golden Phœnix. "His

21

slightest wish it is my delight to honor."

And so they separated, lest spies discover them and bear tales. But he came again the next night and the next, and always they spoke of their love—as though by speaking of love they might forget the awful shadow which hung over them. Never did Golden Phœnix complain of her lot. She was her country's daughter and knew its inexorable laws. To her there was but one thing to do. However it might trouble the heart and soul of Ming Te, he must in the end decide, and the law itself governed his decision—and there was no escape.

From his Grand Councilor he learned that Ma Su— sure that His Majesty would not destroy the woman he loved—had agreed to abide by His Majesty's decision. In Ming Te's mind a plan began to form.

On the morning of the tenth day, a nation in arms awaited the words of Ming Te almost breathlessly.

His Majesty was calm and regal as he sat on his throne to receive the Grand Councilor and the Ministers who spoke with the voice of the people.

"Has Your Majesty decided?" asked the Grand Councilor, when the grim silence of waiting could be borne no longer.

"I have decided," replied Ming Te, "but there are still questions to ask before rendering judgment."

"We will answer them, Your Majesty, if we are capable."

"Is it true that Ma Su will abide by my decision in the matter?"

"It is true, Your Majesty."

"Is it law that when a man is punished for treason, all his family must suffer with him?"

"It is the law, Your Majesty."

"Is it true that whosoever causes the death of the Emperor must suffer in Purgatory for ninety and nine years?"

"It is likewise true, Your Majesty."

For a long moment His Majesty bowed his head in thought, while his Ministers tensely waited, kneeling there with heads bowed—as, outside throughout the country, His Majesty could visualize the millions of his people, waiting, too. Then Ming Te raised his head. He seemed not in doubt as to the words of judgment he must speak.

"Then hearken to me, your Emperor," he said. "It is decreed that Ma Su be decapitated, and all his family destroyed with him!"

There for a moment he left it.

"Her Majesty will be ordered to commit suicide!" went on Ming Te after a moment.

The Ministers, on their knees, began to sway to and

fro.

"His Majesty is mighty!" they muttered. "He sacrifices his all for the good of his people! O mightiest of all rulers!"

"It is further decreed that my son shall also be slain!"

"What, Your Majesty? Your Majesty's son is the Imperial Heir! He must live to rule after Your Majesty, and to worship at Your Majesty's grave!"

"He is the grandson of Ma Su!" replied Ming Te. "I destroy the root with the branch, the cub with the tiger. It is the law. My people have spoken!"

Consternation fled through the ranks of the Ministers. The Grand Councilor's eyes blazed. His hands trembled as though with the palsy.

"It is madness, Your Majesty," he cried.

"My son is grandson of Ma Su and must die with him!" came inexorably from the lips of Ming Te. "My people know the law and have invoked it!"

"But Your Majesty's son will be the next Emperor!"

"He is not yet Emperor, and his destruction will cause no souls to suffer ninety and nine years!"

The Ministers could find nothing to answer His Majesty, and for once even the Grand Councilor was empty of words.

"My son is Ma Su's grandson!" thundered Ming Te. "Is it not true?"

"It is true, Your Majesty!"

"If my people demanded—instead of the life of Golden Phœnix and the life of Ma Su and all his family—my life, and I laid it down, what would it mean to my people?"

"They would never dare!" cried the Grand Councilor. "The hosts of China demand justice for Ma Su and his family. If they demanded the life of Your Majesty, and it were given them—then all the people of China, after death, would suffer ninety and nine years of torment!"

"Yet," said Ming Te, "this they demand of me—and it shall be given! My son is Ma Su's grandson. According to the dynastic law, since Ma Su is a traitor, all his family must be punished with him—thus destroying my son! And I give myself up to my people, upon their express demand, to be decapitated—or to commit suicide, as they wish!"

"But they do not make this demand of Your Majesty! All China would be guilty of treason, and of violence against the person of the Son of Heaven!"

"It is for them to decide. I have decreed according to their wishes!"

"But Your Majesty is not of the family of Ma Su!"

"Is my son not his grandson?"

"He is!"

"Is he not also my son?"

"He is, Your Majesty!"

"Is my son not also of my family?"

"He is, Your Majesty!"

"Could my son be a member of my family, and a member of the family of Ma Su—and yet Ma Su be no member of my family, nor I a member of his? Through Ma Su's grandson, my son, I am a member of the family of Ma Su—and must be destroyed with him, with Golden Phœnix, and the Imperial Heir! My people have spoken. I have decreed with the authority of the Throne!"

"But," gasped the Grand Councilor, "Your Majesty's decree dooms all China to Purgatory for ninety and nine years, because all China has forced this judgment from Your Majesty!"

For the first time Ming Te smiled.

"I have issued the decree my people cried for. I only await their pleasure. Further decision rests with them. It is my final judgment, and I make no other!"

When the people of the Middle Kingdom heard the words of the Emperor they marveled that so much wisdom dwelt in their young ruler, and they quickly decreed that Ma Su, that maker of discord, should be banished from the country forever. They likewise decreed

"Ming Te!" she cried. "Beloved!"

that the lovely Golden Phœnix, who had proved herself willing to lay down her life for the kingdom's welfare, should return in all honor to the eager arms of her lord and master.

So Golden Phœnix, in resplendent robes of state, came back to Ming Te. As she swayed gracefully toward the Emperor, she seemed to him more beautiful than ever before, her pale face illumined by glowing eyes beneath brows as delicate as slender leaves of the willow.

"Ming Te!" she cried. "Beloved!"

And as he caught her to his heart, Ming Te murmured:

"You are in very truth my Precious Pearl among women. Never again shall we be parted, Golden Phœnix."

The Emperor's words came true, for Ming Te ruled for forty and seven years and his Empress with him, so that they grew old peacefully and wonderfully, side by side—and died with hands tightly clasped together, on the same day.

And his son ruled afterward in the place of his father, Ming Te.

LUSTROUS JADE

LUSTROUS JADE

HE rising sun sent its golden rays through the window of the bedroom of Lustrous Jade. The little teahouse maiden stirred in her sleep and sighed. A lattice divided the soft rays of the sun, so that the *kong* upon which Lustrous Jade slept was dappled with dancing lances of light and shadow. A fragile hand rested on the embroidered coverlets, like a lotus blossom on the bosom of a dreamy lake.

Upon the wrist of the sleeper a bracelet of carved jade received the cool caresses of the sunbeams of morning and returned them green-tinted with new beauty. Again the maiden stirred and lazily opened eyes that were all but hidden under lashes black as midnight and shapely as the wings of ebon butterflies. Lustrous Jade turned easily and gazed at the door of her bedroom, which she left open during the hours of night so that all the faint twittering of drowsy birds and the earthy smell of growing things might lull her to sleep, and that her room might be filled with the incense of the garden she loved.

Lustrous Jade saw no happiness in the dawning day,

even though the birds were all a-twitter with joy because the sun was rising in golden splendor over their garden. The odor of many flowers was in the maiden's nostrils, and through all her being she felt the urge to joy and life—but still she sighed. Her eyes fell upon the jade bracelet on her wrist and musingly followed all its shapely convolutions. A gorgeous trinket it was, fashioned like a tiny green dragon with green flames coming from its flaring nostrils. To others such a creature might suggest some fearful nightmare figure; but to Lustrous Jade it symbolized the past, when her father had been a high official at court and the world had been a joyous place in which to live.

Long ago her father had been exiled. His estates confiscated, he had been forbidden to take his family with him into banishment. Lustrous Jade and her elder brother, Ching San, had been left alone to bear life's intolerable burdens. The Emperor whose Imperial Decree had banished their father was long since dead, and his son ruled in his stead. Ching San served the new Emperor as a common soldier, because the decree of banishment had said that none of the household of the disgraced man might ever again hold a post of honor in the government. So Ching San was in the ranks, when he might have been a general; and Lustrous Jade, desperately seeking surcease from goading poverty, was a teahouse maiden. She possessed nothing save the tea-house and the bracelet of jade which the old Emperor had given her the day she was born. That had been when her father was honored and respected at court—before the lying tongues of enemies and false friends had destroyed his hopes and sent him out of China forever.

Merely a symbol, that green bracelet, of past glories whose shadows still hovered over Lustrous Jade and made her sad.

And now she must manage her teahouse alone, for she was no longer able to pay even the tiny fee of a maid to serve those who came to enjoy the tea she brewed and the cakes baked by her own hands. To her, who had never during her life with her father known the necessity of labor, these burdens seemed unbelievably heavy.

Lustrous Jade slipped from the *kong* and began her toilet for the day. Her black hair she combed back so that her oval face was framed in its long ebon glory, and in her glistening locks she placed jasmine flowers from her garden. Then she brought forth the round mirror that had no handle but silken tassels at the back which might be entwined in her fingers as she held the glass up before her. She hung the mirror over the little table which held fragile jars and bottles. Carefully, as though it had been a regal ceremony, she darkened her eyebrows until they were blacker still—dusky little wings all spread for flight. Her delicate nails she tinted with color from the heart of a lady's-slipper from the sunny garden.

When she had completed her toilet, Lustrous Jade looked like one of the flowers that bloomed and nodded in her own garden.

From the tearoom came the musical tinkling of the tiny bell which announced the first visitor of the morning, and Lustrous Jade sighed again. Those who came to her did not understand that she was the daughter of a once mighty house. They were usually boisterous and rude and given much to talk such as had never been heard in her father's house.

But Lustrous Jade must serve her guest. Hesitantly, wishing that it were not necessary, hoping almost that the visitor would tire of waiting and withdraw before she reached the tearoom, Lustrous Jade swayed on her tiny feet toward the door.

The room she entered was gorgeous, even for a teahouse. The panels were darkly tinted. Dragons and lotus flowers intermingled in delicate designs from tiled floor to fluted ceiling. Little painted people in the costumes of ancient times made genuflections to one another on the walls, their faces always happy, as though in olden times there had been nothing to make people sad.

Lustrous Jade loved most the panel where Confucius spoke compassionately to a group of solemn men in wondrous gowns of silks and satins—while above his head, behind the cloud that drifted over the group like a gently falling white mantle, a procession of little fairies, hands clasped in elfin circle, were dancing in the moon.

Slowly Lustrous Jade forced herself to observe her early-morning visitor and was stricken with surprise. He was like no other who had ever come to her teahouse. His fingernails were as well cared for as her own. His robe was as rich as any her father had ever worn; but of course it could not have been a court robe, for no courtier would ever come to her humble teahouse. The stranger rose to meet Lustrous Jade and clasped his hands together within his voluminous sleeves to make his ceremonial genuflections. Again Lustrous Jade was mystified—for usually those who came to the teahouse were too ill-mannered to be courteous to a teahouse maiden. Her heart fluttered with pleasure. For a moment she felt as though she were once again in her father's house, bowing to one of his illustrious guests.

"My humble teahouse is honored by your august presence," she began diffidently.

As he seated himself again, the newcomer did not answer, but from behind his jeweled fan he regarded Lustrous Jade with an air of interest and friendliness. His black eyes, which seemed to look right into the heart of the maiden and to set it fluttering, gazed upon her with courteous approval.

Lustrous Jade went to bring his tea and cakes. He still said nothing, and Lustrous Jade, as became a shy maiden of the Middle Kingdom, retreated to the screen before her bedroom door, from behind which she peered with even greater curiosity upon her guest.

"What gentle wind brought him to my teahouse?" she asked herself. "He is not like the others, that is plain. And why should my poor heart flutter so, merely because he is here?"

When the stranger had finished his tea, Lustrous Jade did not like to speak of money. She had been gently reared and regarded money as merely the medium of barter for coolies and tradesmen. But the stranger extended payment for the tea and cakes, and Lustrous Jade, shyly wondering why her cheeks were flushed, put forth her hand to accept the money. For a long moment payment was delayed, until Lustrous Jade raised her eyes to the stranger.

But he was not gazing at her. His eyes were fixed upon the bracelet on her wrist. Lustrous Jade began to tremble, unaccountably afraid. She fancied she could read the thoughts in the mind of the stranger. That jade dragon bracelet could have come from but one place—the Throne! And this man must be wondering how the humble maiden of a teahouse chanced to possess a piece so delicately wrought.

Rousing himself suddenly, her guest exchanged courteous genuflections with Lustrous Jade, laid the money in her hand, and departed. It was lavish payment, she noted, as much as she usually received in an entire day from all her guests combined. The stranger had not spoken a word—yet the heart of Lustrous Jade beat tumultuously, and the day seemed long after he had left.

That he was handsome, as handsome even as Ching San, her elder brother, she had noted; yet she had seen many handsome men who had not caused her heart to beat so loudly. That he was richly garbed she had also observed, but she had seen many another garbed as richly. That he was of illustrious birth was plainly evident; still her own estate had been a high one. Why, then, was she so concerned with this stranger?

Next morning he came again, early as before, when there was none in the teahouse save himself and Lustrous Jade. After his genuflections he bade her good-morning, and his voice was low-pitched and musical.

But when Lustrous Jade brought him his tea and cakes, his eyes fell again upon the jade bracelet.

"If you would not consider it a question unseemly and discourteous," he said, " I would ask you concerning that bracelet of jade. It is an Imperial Gift perhaps. Will you not tell me about it?"

Lustrous Jade was trembling. Why should the stranger be interested in this symbol of the past days of her family? Given her at her birth, she wore it always because it reminded her of days when she had been happy. But she must answer, as to evade answering might create suspicion, and one never knew what stories might be carried to the court.

"It is from the Throne, Illustrious One," she said in a low voice. "It was bestowed upon my father by His Majesty, when I was born, as a token of long life and prosperity. Will you deign to notice the inscription, done by the hand of one of His Majesty's master craftsmen? The symbol of long life, '*shou*,' and the symbol of prosperity, '*lu*,' with my name, Lustrous Jade, set between them."

"Lustrous Jade," murmured her guest, rising and bowing as though this had been their first meeting. "It is a beautiful name; yet it is not as beautiful as you are, if this humble person may make bold to speak what his heart and his eyes tell him is true. But you say His

Majesty bestowed this exquisite piece of jade when you were born. Yet His Majesty is himself scarce older than you! Surely here is a mystery!"

"I meant the father of our Emperor who today sits upon the Dragon Throne."

"But it is beyond the comprehension of this thrice ignorant person that one so favored of His Majesty should be a teahouse maiden!"

Then, as though realizing that he had asked too much, had perhaps been discourteous, the stranger made haste to rise and bow in humble apology for having dared to transgress the august proprieties by asking questions and betraying unmannerly curiosity.

His words had recalled her unhappiness to Lustrous Jade. Sympathy and compassion were in the eyes of her guest, and, scarcely realizing what she was doing, she found herself telling this man of her sorrows.

"Once," she said, "none might have guessed that I would ever become a teahouse maiden, suffering the rude banter of all who come to eat and drink. My father was a favorite at the court of the Emperor, loved and respected by all who knew him. Because of his high place he had many enemies, some of whom spoke with the soft words of friends. These played him false and carried lying tales to the Emperor. In the end His Majesty believed the stories, which my father was too proud to deny. My father was banished, and as my mother had died shortly after my birth, my elder brother, Ching San, and I were left alone to sorrow for our father who could never again return to the Middle Kingdom. My brother became a common soldier—all official rank being forever denied him as part of our father's punishment—and I became a teahouse maiden."

The guest was all sympathy.

"But surely," he said, "if His Majesty, the Young Emperor, knew this story, he, too, would believe! Someone should intercede for you so that you might be received in audience to tell the truth."

"It is too late," said Lustrous Jade, something of bitterness in her voice. "My father has been silent since his banishment to Turkestan. We fear that years ago his proud heart broke, and that he must have joined his honorable ancestors."

Suddenly Lustrous Jade remembered that it was not proper to discuss these matters with an utter stranger. Her fair cheeks flushed swiftly, and she prepared to retreat.

"I should not have spoken," she said in a low voice, "for my words might seem disloyal to his Departed Majesty, when they are not so intended. My family has always been loyal to the throne, and I should not speak of these matters to one whose name is hidden from me."

"Stay!" implored the stranger. "And since I know your name, Lustrous Jade, you may call me Liu Pe."

So Lustrous Jade lost her fear of Liu Pe, who came often to the teahouse, and she even sat at his table when there were no other guests. He spoke of far places in the Middle Kingdom, and the maiden knew that he had traveled widely and that his heart was filled with compassion for the country's lowly and impoverished. When he looked at Lustrous Jade his eyes shone with approval, and he delighted to make her laugh with him over little things. As they talked, Lustrous Jade forgot that she was merely a teahouse maiden, and remembered instead the days when she had been the daughter of a high official of the court, the equal of any person in all the great Empire.

But one morning Ching San, her elder brother, returned from duty with the army to spend a few hours with his adored sister. He was all courtesy to Liu Pe and performed the genuflections decreed by custom with all the grace of his own high birth—for one never gave offense to a guest of the house.

After Liu Pe had left, however, Ching San's face became a thundercloud.

"How is it, Little Sister," he asked, "that I find you laughing and making speech with this gentleman who cannot honorably be interested in a mere teahouse maiden? Who is he? Why does he come here to hold speech with you?"

For the first time Lustrous Jade realized how her growing friendship with Liu Pe, so harmless and beautiful, might seem to others. Ching San, of course, loved her with all his heart. He must know what was right and proper for her.

"The gentleman's honorable name is Liu Pe," she told Ching San, "and he is great and good. He does not laugh at me, nor is he ever boisterous as are others who come for tea and cakes. With him I forget that I am but a teahouse maiden and that you are only a common soldier. Sometimes I even forget that our father is gone."

"But he is of illustrious birth, and we are sunk to low estate. How can his intentions toward you be honorable, Little Sister? Men of his rank do not take wives from the teahouse."

"He is but a friend, and one who makes me happy! There have been no words spoken of marriage!"

"That is even more terrifying," said Ching San gloomily. "It were better that he did speak of marriage. He must not come here again, Little Sister."

"But, Elder Brother," Lustrous Jade's eyes were brimming with unshed tears, "I enjoy speech with him, and we are happy together. There is nothing between

42

us but friendship. He brings me joy during the endless days when you are gone from me. How can we ask him not to come again? It would be an insult to one of great family. We dare not offend those who come to buy."

"Why did he come here in the beginning, Little Sister?"

"That I know not, Elder Brother. He has often told me that he goes everywhere, because he is interested in the welfare of the people and wishes to see how they live. So I believe he came here first by chance."

"And afterward?"

"Because—perhaps because—he enjoys being with me and speaking of those things which interest us both."

"He must not come again," insisted Ching San. "And you, Little Sister, must find a way of telling him that will not give him offense."

But how could she do it? How could she hurt this man who had made her laugh for the first time since her father had gone? Why must she find a good and gentle friend only to lose him because of rigid custom? Why should not a teahouse maiden be the friend of a man like Liu Pe? Had she herself not been the daughter of a great official? How was Lustrous Jade of the teahouse different from Lustrous Jade to whom an Emperor had given a dragon bracelet?

Life seemed monstrously unfair, and all the sunlight

had vanished with the words of Ching San—yet she knew that his words accorded with ancient and honored custom. So when Liu Pe came the following morning, she made her heart strong to tell him that he must not return.

But when she tried to speak of this, words failed her. A great hand seemed to clasp itself about her heart, and she stood mute before Liu Pe as he made his genuflections of greeting. Startled and dismayed, Liu Pe looked at her. Lustrous Jade did not know that she was crying.

Then Liu Pe spoke softly, compassionately, and beckoned her to a seat near him at the table.

"Even your tears, Lustrous Jade," he told her, "are precious beyond price. They are pearls which move in regal procession down your golden cheeks. When you weep, you are more lovely than the dawn. But though tears make you even more beautiful, you must not weep, Lustrous Jade. Tell me why you are unhappy."

Quickly she tried to dry her tears, but they only flowed faster. The words she knew she must utter would not come.

"Lustrous Jade," said her guest, "there are many things I must tell you. I have heard and have believed the story of your family. I have made sure that His Majesty, the Emperor, learned the truth as it fell from your lips. But there is more. I have often told you that

44

you are beautiful, but I have never yet told you how I worship you, Lustrous Jade! I love you with all the soul of me!"

Lustrous Jade looked in amazement at Liu Pe. Could this marvelous thing be happening to her?

"According to the custom I should ask my father to send a matchmaker to your brother, Lustrous Jade," continued Liu Pe. "But my father has joined his honorable ancestors; and, before I send formally to propose for your hand, I wish you to know that to me you are altogether lovely and that my very heart cries out for you. I am humble before you, beloved, because your beauty blinds me and makes me afraid. When you walk, you sway with the grace of a willow tree in a gentle breeze—entrancing the heart of one who loves you. The birds descend from the skies to pay homage to you, Lustrous Jade, and even the brilliance of the moon pales beside your beauty. I am far too lowly to aspire to your love."

The heart of Lustrous Jade was beating like the wings of tiny birds against the cage that imprisons them. Her eyes were bright, and her parted lips were red as ripe cherries. These words of Liu Pe! How could she answer them as she wished?

At this moment her brother joined them, and Lustrous Jade, in happy confusion, fled from the tearoom,

leaving Liu Pe with Ching San. The stranger immediately addressed Ching San.

"Honorable Sir," he said, "I love your sister, and,
though she has never told me, I believe that she loves
me, too. With your permission I shall send the matchmaker to you to arrange a marriage."

"She is only a teahouse maiden," replied Ching San.

"She is your father's daughter," countered Liu Pe,
"and evil fortune alone has cast her down. Will you receive the matchmaker?"

"But all that we know of you, August Stranger," protested Ching San, "is that you have told us to call you
Liu Pe. Everywhere that I have asked about you I have
received only evasive answers. Besides, we are poor. We
could not even give the customary present to the matchmaker."

Liu Pe smiled, and his smile was so winning that even
Ching San was persuaded for the moment, although he
still knew that no man of exalted family ever married
a teahouse maiden.

So the matchmaker came, and to him Ching San
poured out the troubles of his heart. He spoke of their
poverty and of his doubts concerning a marriage between Lustrous Jade and Liu Pe. And even as he spoke
he was thinking that Liu Pe must be even greater than

they had fancied, for the matchmaker he had chosen wore a robe that was rich and full of costly colors.

But when Ching San made an end of his many objections, the matchmaker only smiled, made deep obeisance, and continued talking. After a while, however, Ching San sent him away, telling him that the matter was impossible. Then Liu Pe came in his stead.

"If it is only the seeming difference in our stations," he ended his argument with Ching San, "then I beg you, as you love your sister, have her make ready her marriage gown. I shall send the bridal chair on the day and hour which seem auspicious after I have consulted the book of good and evil portent."

Ching San found himself helpless to refuse as Liu Pe, bowing and smiling, quitted the teahouse. So he told Lustrous Jade and later smiled—a bit dubiously, perhaps—to hear her singing as she brewed the tea and made the little cakes that she need never make again after she became the bride of Liu Pe.

The passing days seemed long, for Liu Pe did not come again in the early morning; but Lustrous Jade made ready her bridal gown with fingers that fairly flew. Was she not preparing herself for the man she loved? She, too, had studied the book of good and evil portent and thus knew on what day the bridal chair must come. Then she would be certain about the rank of the family of Liu Pe. She could tell by the color of the chair and by the number of bearers.

At last the day came—and Lustrous Jade, her heart beating quickly with mingled joy and fright, was ready. Many times as she waited she went to the door to look down the way by which Liu Pe had always come, knowing that from that direction would come the chair to bear her to her future lord's home.

Hours passed, and the bridal chair did not come—at least, not her bridal chair. But—what was this? Excitedly she called her brother. Ching San came, and Lustrous Jade pointed down the way.

"Truly a marvelous omen, Elder Brother!" she cried. "For His Majesty, the Young Emperor, must be taking a bride today. Does it not portend good fortune that Liu Pe sends the bridal chair for me on the same day that His Majesty weds? I wonder what princess of the Imperial Clan His Majesty has chosen."

It was a gorgeous procession that wound along the way that led past the teahouse of Lustrous Jade. There was a great sedan chair borne by sixty chair-bearers. This bridal chair was as yellow as the sun whose rays it reflected in little lancets of gold. The bearers were robed in great richness, as became servants of the court.

48

There were scores of outriders, court officials mounted on curvetting Mongolian ponies, all gaily caparisoned, their flowing manes ruffled by the breeze. The officials wore the buttons of high rank on their caps and carried themselves proudly as they rode—for they were the truly great of the Empire.

On came the procession, while brother and sister marveled at the great good fortune that had caused the Emperor to take a bride on the same day that Lustrous Jade was to journey to the house of her lord. Now they understood why the bridal chair of Liu Pe was late in coming. Even Liu Pe, whatever his greatness, must make way for the Emperor, so that His Majesty might use the serpentine road for his own wedding procession.

Then the joy in the hearts of Ching San and Lustrous Jade gave way to clutching fear—for the Emperor's bridal chair of gold was turning in at the gate of the teahouse courtyard! Old terrors came rushing back. The Decree which had sent their father into exile had stipulated that none of his family might ever hold office of trust or honor in the Empire—and this must mean that His Majesty had heard of Lustrous Jade's impending marriage to Liu Pe and was forbidding it. Liu Pe must be mighty, and Lustrous Jade—under the shadow of disgrace—no fit mate for him. Yet why did

49

His Majesty send a bridal chair instead of the Imperial Courier?

The great golden procession following the bridal chair came to rest outside the courtyard. An official stepped from one of the many sedan chairs. As he approached, his face stern, his manner unbending, he unrolled a yellow parchment.

"Let Lustrous Jade and her brother Ching San," came the melodious voice of the official, "kneel in their courtyard to hear the Imperial Decree of His Majesty, the Emperor!"

Their hearts like stones in their breasts, their world once more toppling, brother and sister knelt and kowtowed, according to the custom for recipients of Imperial Decrees. The language of the official was soft and sonorous, but to the two hearers most interested the flowing words spelled disaster.

Lustrous Jade, on the day set for her marriage to Liu Pe, was being bidden to the Imperial Court to become the bride of the Young Emperor! The words of the reader continued, but Lustrous Jade scarcely heard them. She only knew that they were barring her forever from Liu Pe, for none might refuse to obey His Majesty. Lustrous Jade must travel to the palace in the golden bridal chair, and, though she would become

Empress, her heart was heavy as lead in her breast—for she loved only Liu Pe.

"Rise, Illustrious Lady, and enter the Imperial Chair!"

Hearkening to the words of the Royal Courier, Lustrous Jade knew that for her the world had ended. But how could she go with never a word for Liu Pe? He would seek her always, and his heart would be broken.

"Grant me but a moment for a word with my brother," she begged the Courier. "We never hoped for such honor. . . . We . . . we would speak apart. . . ."

With a strained smile the Courier gave permission.

"You must make haste, Illustrious Lady," he said, bowing deeply as though Lustrous Jade were already Empress. "His Majesty is not to be kept waiting."

Quickly brother and sister turned toward the tea-house. There were tears on the pale cheeks of Lustrous Jade.

"Why must this terrible thing happen, today of all days?" she sobbed.

"Perhaps," said Ching San gently, "His Majesty only tries to make amends for the wrong done our father. This is the highest honor he can bestow—and you will be the greatest lady in the Middle Kingdom."

"I do not desire greatness! I wish only for Liu Pe.

51

Do you think if the Emperor knew that today I was to wed Liu Pe he would withdraw his Decree?"

"Perhaps," replied Ching San doubtfully. "But his wrath might fall upon you and upon Liu Pe."

"Then you think there is no hope? If only I might seek help from Liu Pe!"

They entered the tearoom, and suddenly Liu Pe, whom none had seen enter, was there before them—a grave Liu Pe. He rose and bowed deeply to Lustrous Jade.

"I have heard," he said. "And I have seen. His Majesty is making amends."

"But I cannot become his Empress," sobbed Lustrous Jade. "I love only you, Liu Pe. I do not wish to be Empress!"

"His Majesty will give you palaces, serving maids without number, and eunuchs to obey your slightest commands. He will give you the wealth of the Empire."

"You knew? Is that why your bridal chair did not come?"

"I myself told your story to His Majesty. He promised to make amends. He is doing so."

"But if I do not wish to be Empress—"

"There is no disobeying the Imperial Decree. There is nothing you may not have."

"I want nothing His Majesty can give me—save you,

beloved, even though we are compelled to dwell in a hovel with only rough rice to eat!"

"Alas! There is nothing I can do. But always I shall carry your fragile beauty in my heart and shall love you beyond this life."

"If only you had not believed my story and had said nothing to the Emperor!" cried Lustrous Jade. "I am sure that my illustrious father is long since dead and that this belated honor could not matter to him."

"There is more, Lustrous Jade," said Liu Pe softly. "I said His Majesty wished to make full amends. Couriers were sent throughout Turkestan, whither your father was banished. He is not dead, but living. Even now he has returned and is again a court official. But your father is old and could not come for you now. He waits for you at the palace."

"Then you knew, even before now, what His Majesty intended and did nothing to dissuade him?" cried Lustrous Jade.

"There is still more," said Liu Pe, his voice low, his face troubled. "Today your brother, Ching San, becomes a Governor of a Province!"

For a full moment Lustrous Jade and Ching San stared at Liu Pe. How great was this man! Everything he had done for Lustrous Jade at court had but put her further from him. How could Lustrous Jade forsake a man who loved her so deeply that he sacrificed himself for her sake—giving her to another.

"Hear me, Liu Pe," she said. "I want none but you, and though death be the penalty for disobedience of the Imperial Decree, I shall wed none but you!"

"Have you thought what your refusal may mean to your father and to Ching San?"

"Take no thought for me," cried Ching San. "I would rather remain a common soldier all the days of my life than that Lustrous Jade should have another moment of unhappiness. And I am sure I voice the wishes of my father, too. He has spent years in exile without murmuring. To make Lustrous Jade happy, he would return without complaint!"

"No! No!" said Lustrous Jade. "I am utterly selfish. The Imperial Decree must be obeyed. My father must spend his last years in the land he loves. And you, Elder Brother, must accept your appointment—there is no other way."

A smile transfigured the face of Liu Pe.

"Now, Lustrous Jade," he said softly, "I know that you love me greatly. I know, too, that your heart is loyal and great and that you are good beyond the goodness of women. I am humbled with sorrow that I have deceived you, for I should have known. Do not frown,

54

beloved, when I make abject confession—that His Majesty's bridal chair is also the bridal chair of Liu Pe!"

As he spoke Liu Pe flung back his robe to disclose beneath a gorgeous golden robe emblazoned with silken clouds and ocean waves of satin, and having marvelously wrought in the center of the breast the Imperial Yellow Dragon of the Middle Kingdom, which only the Emperor might wear!

Instantly, like people stricken, Lustrous Jade and Ching San dropped to their knees to kowtow to His Majesty—who had been Liu Pe. But he lifted them quickly, a hand on the arm of each.

"It is I, Lustrous Jade," said His Majesty, "who should kowtow to you. For to me you are all that is great under heaven. Touch my cheeks with your fragile hands, Little Empress, so that I shall know by your caress that you love me as you loved me yesterday when I was Liu Pe and you were a teahouse maiden."

With a sob of joy Lustrous Jade swayed toward the waiting arms of her lord, while Ching San looked on as one turned to stone. It was Liu Pe who roused him to realization of the greatest good fortune that could have come to anyone in the Empire.

"Ching San," said His Majesty, "bid the Grand Councilor make ready the bridal chair for Lustrous

55

Jade."

And never before had the sun shone so brightly upon the Middle Kingdom as on the day that Lustrous Jade became Empress—and wed at the same time the man she loved with all her heart.

BLACK DRAGON MOUNTAIN

BLACK DRAGON MOUNTAIN

ULL of years and greatly wise was Duke Lan Chi, ruler of the little duchy of Black Dragon Mountain. His subjects loved him and he loved them—perhaps too much, for there were certain of his nobles who took advantage of his kindness and hospitality. One vanity Duke Lan Chi had—he was proud of his beard, which was longer than the longest beard of any of his nobles. It was a magnificent version of the usual beard of five strands—two of which hung like lace from the upper lip—one from the chin, and one below each ear. When he was pleased or angry he stroked his beard with his long fingernails. But he was angry so seldom that his duchy was the happiest in all the Middle Kingdom.

The brightest jewel in all Black Dragon Mountain was the duke's daughter Yung Shi, Eternal Joy. Even the magic words of the Classics or the rhetoric of the Literati could not do full justice to the beauty of Eternal Joy at seventeen. Some of her gorgeous gowns had been created by the aged tailors of Black Dragon Mountain—and were beautiful to behold. Their embroideries were of the deep blue of sea and sky or the

59

whiteness of snow, so real that one who looked upon them could almost hear surf on the shore, see dim stars in the sky or feel the chill of snow. Some of her gowns even came from the Forbidden City where they had been created by the inspired hands of tailors at Her Majesty's court. The shoes of Yung Shi were so small they could be hidden in the most fragile of teacups. They were studded with gems until they twinkled in the light like clusters of little stars, only less brilliant than other stars sprinkling her headdress.

Eternal Joy was small and delicate. Her lips were curves of scarlet, her eyes as deeply black as midnight, her eyebrows tiny ebon moths which fluttered forever about the lights of gladness in her eyes. It was little wonder the old duke loved her and stroked his beard so ecstatically when he thought of her; and never was there a moment when her picture was not in his heart.

As she made her genuflections of filial piety on a certain momentous morning, he said to her:

"Eternal Joy, for all the sweet years of your life you have been a delight to the heart of your father. And once long ago, before you were born, I wished for a boy! It was well that the gods did not grant me my wish, for then I should never have looked upon your golden brilliance to be blinded by it! Your mother mounted the Dragon Throne on High and filled my heart with sorrow; but immediately she returned to me in you. I can see her in your eyes, in the royal manner of your walk. And when you speak I can hear her voice."

How well they understood each other, the old duke and his daughter. Never, after the Chinese custom, could he speak words to her to hide his real meaning, for she could look straight into his heart no matter the words he spoke.

"Does my father speak to me as though he were a lover?" she asked him softly, then laughed as she noted his quick confusion. "Ah, my father, if only a bridegroom who would be like you would come for me. When I dream of a bridegroom he always looks like you, my august father, save that he is young and wears no beard."

"You do not like my beard?" the duke asked with pretended anger.

"Of course, but a beard so long should belong to one of great wisdom, and you have often told me I should not expect too great wisdom in the young bridegroom who will come."

The duke sighed heavily.

"Little Eternal Joy," he said, "that is the matter of which I must speak with you. Stand near me, daughter. Give me your hand. It is like satin and so small it is almost lost in mine. The man who is worthy to hold this little hand as I do must needs be more than a man, almost a god! Yet soon, my daughter, the time must come when I too shall mount the Dragon Throne on High. Then you will be the sole ruler of Black Dragon Mountain and many will come to seek you as bride. But remember this, Eternal Joy; when I have gone from you there will be few in all the Middle Kingdom who will possess the wealth that will be yours. And it is the dearest wish of my heart that your bridegroom shall be worthy."

"If he must be one of the nobles," she whispered, "I like none of them."

"It is my desire to see you wedded to some good man ere I go," replied the duke, "for it is not good for a maiden to rule alone."

"Father," she replied, "I pray you may have many years to rule Black Dragon Mountain ere you join my mother on the Dragon Throne. Surely there is no need for haste. Let me be happy alone for yet a little while."

"What do you wish, Eternal Joy? Always it is my pride to grant your slightest wish."

"It is the season of the year when bright-plumed birds abound in the woods on the mountainside. Grant permission that I go forth in the morning with all my retinue to have a holiday in the hills. We shall go to hunt pheasants."

62

"It is not like you to wish to slay," began Duke Lan Chi.

"I shall hunt the gorgeous birds only to bring them hither with me, alive, and give them homes, so that their marvelous plumage will add to the brilliance of the court of my august father," replied Eternal Joy.

Duke Lan Chi stroked his beard even more strongly than was his usual wont, because he was more pleased than ever with his daughter. It never seemed possible that he could be more pleased with her than he was, yet always he surprised himself. And each time he told himself that the bridegroom whom he would one day choose must be perfect.

To be sure that no harm befall Eternal Joy he sent with her on the pheasant hunt most of his palace guard, besides soldiers, servants, serving maids, ladies-in-waiting and her old nurse Li Nai Ma. All were garbed in gorgeous costumes of the hunt. For Eternal Joy the journey into the mountains should be a holiday, a ceremonial day no less grand in its trappings than the days when Duke Lan Chi held audience with his nobles whose robes rivaled the brilliance of the sun.

There were scores of chair-bearers, and the sedan chair which bore the duke's daughter forth on the hunt was so large it was as though her own chamber had been changed to a sedan chair, placed on the backs of coolies and sent into the mountains. From the broad steps of the palace Duke Lan Chi watched the joy of his life depart with a smile of happiness on her lips.

"I pray to the gods," he whispered to himself, "that never in life will she be less happy than she is at this moment."

The sun struck facets of light from the gilded roof of the sedan chair which carried Eternal Joy forth on the hunt. It turned to a deeper brown the broad backs of the smiling coolies who supported the weight of her chair. Proudly held were the heads of her outriders who surrounded the chair on curvetting Mongolian ponies. Proud too were the ponies, tossing their heads so that their manes were like banners, their hoofbeats like the thrumming of drums, their eyes as bright as live coals. For even the ponies knew how precious was this burden the coolies carried to the pheasant hunt and were proud to accompany the bright cavalcade.

The sun was high in the heavens which held under their blue bowl the broad lands of the Middle Kingdom when the cavalcade came to a halt in the high mountains. Eternal Joy peered forth from behind the curtains of her chair and asked why they had paused.

"Here the way is exceedingly narrow and dangerous and riders cannot meet and pass," explained a noble who rode beside the chair. "Yet yonder is one who dares to ask by what right we command him to make way. He is as proud as though he himself were a duke. Yet his clothing is poor and he wears no jewels, not even so much as a button of rank on his hat. When we tell him that it is Yung Shi, daughter of the Duke of Black Dragon Mountain who seeks to pass, he merely smiles as though it were a jest and refuses to move aside or to go back ahead of us the way he came. But the matter is simple. We have but to strike off his head and proceed.

A little smile touched the red lips of Eternal Joy.

"He is a young man?" she asked.

"Very young and lacking in wisdom," the noble replied.

"He is handsome, this proud one?"

"Very handsome, but even coolies are sometimes handsome."

"It is my wish that this young man who is so rude and handsome and smiles so freely be brought to me here, that I may see for myself the manner of man who dares to ignore the commands of my father's nobles."

"But," objected the nobles, "you are a young woman and unmarried, and the proprieties—"

"I am Lady Yung Shi," she interrupted, "and how can the proprieties be transgressed if the daughter of a duke condescends to address a commoner? Bid the young man here instantly!"

And so the young man came—smiling. His face was handsomer than she had expected. Erect as a soldier he strode without fear among her father's men-at-arms whom he did not even seem to see. The heart of Eternal Joy began to race swiftly as she looked into his dancing, mischievous eyes. Then her own smile faded. His clothing was not rich, nor bedecked with pearls. He was poor, then,.as the nobles had said.

But when his eyes fell upon the fragile grace and beauty of the little lady of the sedan chair he dropped instantly and most humbly before her, his knees in the dust of the way, his eyes cast down.

"What is the name of one who dares bar the way of the daughter of Duke Lan Chi?" asked Eternal Joy, while her eyes noted the strength of this young man and the beauty of him.

"My despicable name, daughter of Black Dragon Mountain," he replied in a voice that was like music, "is Hu Fo and I am the son of a very old man who lives in the mountains. Most abjectly I perform my genuflections, for when your nobles bade me make way for the daughter of Duke Lan Chi I thought they jested."

She knew there was mirth in his words, for he must have known that none in all Black Dragon Mountain save her father could have sent such a rich cavalcade on a mere pheasant hunt. But her heart warmed toward him for his very jesting.

"The life of this despicable person, gorgeous maiden," he told her, "rests in your fragile hands. Tell me your wishes and I shall heed."

For a moment she hesitated.

"It is my wish," she said at last, "that you walk beside my chair to the place where the cavalcade spends the night."

"But I have a horse."

"You object already? Did you not say that whatever I wished—"

"You doubt my sincerity then? With your permission I will stand. The punishment is just. I will walk beside your chair. But I beg that one of your soldiers may lead my horse."

As they went on into the mountain Hu Fo walked with his hand on the sedan chair borne by the coolies, and held speech with Eternal Joy. Many indeed were the things they had to say to each other. Long ere they reached the hunting lodges of Duke Lan Chi, Eternal Joy knew that her heart would al-

ways thereafter beat faster when she thought of Hu
Fo, and Hu Fo knew that for him life would be all
emptiness if he were never again to see Eternal
Joy.

"It is my further wish," she told him when they
had reached the place where night was to be passed,
"that you return here at sunrise tomorrow and accompany me on the pheasant hunt. And if you know the
mountains well and can travel them at night, remain
now for a time and hold speech with me before you
return to your father."

So at the hunting lodge of the Duke of Lan Chi
they spent many happy hours together and talked
long and much. But when the stars came out and
the mists and shadows of night filled all the ravines,
they scarcely spoke at all. They talked to each other
without words as simply and joyously as though
they addressed each other with all the ancient rhetoric of the Classics. It was late, the nobles were
muttering, and even Li Nai Ma was perturbed when
at last she bade him go. She watched him mount
the white horse he seemed to love so much, and
again she noted, by his carriage and the way he sat
his great steed, how he resembled a soldier of high
rank.

"At sunrise, Hu Fo," she called to him softly.

"At sunrise if I live," he answered with a voice that rang with happiness, "and nothing can happen to me until I have seen you again, nor shall I truly live between this hour and the rising of the sun."

So he rode away into the east, mingling at last with the moonlight which covered the mountains with silver. Eternal Joy entered the mountain dwelling, and all night in her dreams she watched a handsome young man ride away into the moonlight.

"Yes," she whispered, "long ago my father was like Hu Fo."

Long before sunrise a coal black horse was brought for Eternal Joy, for she would ride to the pheasant hunt—and atop the black animal, who seemed to know as well as did the nobles how precious was his burden. Eternal Joy faced the east and awaited the coming of Hu Fo.

Just as lances of gold pierced the black and gray of the east, Hu Fo came again on his white horse, with the rising sun behind him. It was as though he wore the sun's morning rays like a cloak—a cloak that was long and draped even the sides of his snow-white horse.

Bright were the cheeks of Eternal Joy when she

saw him come riding, and bright were her eyes which the rising sun caressed, and joyous her laughter as in welcome she raised above her head the whip of white silk that never would touch the sleek ebon sides of her horse.

"Welcome, Hu Fo!" she called. Behind her the nobles shook their heads and muttered.

He dismounted before her and bent his knees again in the dust; but she bade him mount and ride. During all the day they were side by side and knee to knee. Their laughter echoed through the ravines and played caressingly about the towering crags.

But a shadow crossed his face when, at evening, as they turned to face the sunset, she said:

"My father would be pleased to welcome you at the ducal palace of Black Dragon Mountain."

"It is more than this lowly person could ask, delicate flower of the mountains," he whispered. "But always, though we never meet again, your face will be before my eyes, my hands will be warm with the touch of yours, and your little feet will leave their gentle prints upon my heart. Now I must bid you farewell, Eternal Joy, and beg that you remember me with kindness."

BLACK DRAGON MOUNTAIN

Eternal Joy wondered why she felt no happiness that many gorgeous pheasants went back with the cavalcade when she returned to her father. She told him of Hu Fo—and imagined that she saw a twinkle in his eyes. He stroked his beard furiously, but he did not seem angry and his hand upon her head was very gentle.

"Forget this young man, my daughter," he counseled. "Tonight there shall be a great banquet to celebrate the success of the hunt. And in your honor all the court of Black Dragon Mountain shall garb itself in finest robes."

"Hu Fo seemed amazed at my being mounted, father," she mused aloud, as though she had not heard his words. "He said that he did not think the daughter of a duke should ride a horse."

"I have reared you like a boy in many ways, Eternal Joy," he said softly, "because I have no son to rule after me and you will succeed me in the affairs of Black Dragon Mountain. But are you not happy that there will be a banquet?"

"Whatever makes you happy, august father," she said smiling, "makes me happy, too. But I wish . . ."

"What is it you wish, Eternal Joy?"

"That Hu Fo were a noble!"

Duke Lan Chi merely stroked his beard, but his eyes twinkled.

That night two things happened. Hu Fo came to the banquet and was turned away by the nobles because his clothing lacked in richness and there were no jewels in his hat. And after the banquet Duke Lan Chi passed away in his bed with a smile on his lips and his fingers on his beard—as if at the end some thought had pleased him.

Lady Eternal Joy became ruler of Black Dragon Mountain.

For many days, in accordance with custom, Duke Lan Chi rested in state in his palace, while his nobles, after examining the book of good and evil portent, decided on the date he would journey to the tomb. During all those days Eternal Joy wept softly and could not be comforted. The faithful old Li Nai Ma, nurse of her childhood, tried to soothe her, but could not make her forget her sorrow. She had loved her kindly father with a love beyond words, a love that caused broken sobs that would not end even after all her tears had been wept away.

At last the duke went forth to meet his wife on the Dragon Throne of Heaven and Eternal Joy was left, wan of face and sad beyond measure, to rule in Black Dragon Mountain. She was thankful now that she had been reared almost like a boy, since she could look forward without fear to ruling the subjects who loved her.

"But even though my honored father reared me as a boy," she said to Li Nai Ma, "I am still a girl and my heart is heavy. Have you noticed how the nobles look upon me? They at least do not regard me as a boy!"

"Some of them are young, my precious one," whispered old Li Nai Ma, "and all of them are only less wealthy than was your father Duke Lan Chi. Not one among the nobles but would be honored to seek your hand in marriage, now that you are ruler of the duchy."

And Eternal Joy wept again.

"But they would wed me because I *am* the ruler now, not because they love me. I am wealthier than any of them, or than all of them. How shall I know they do not seek me for my wealth and my power?"

"How does any maiden know the thoughts in the hearts of those who come a-wooing?" replied Li Nai Ma.

Eternal Joy sighed most deeply.

"If only—" she began, then hesitated. "If only

73

Hu Fo were a noble! I know he loves me because I am Eternal Joy, and I love him because he is Hu Fo. What matters power or wealth to either of us when each of us knows that our love is riches beyond our greatest dreams?"

"But he is poor, little daughter of Black Dragon Mountain, and there would be only ill fortune in it. Dry your eyes, Eternal Joy, for tomorrow you must hold your first audience with your nobles."

For a long moment Eternal Joy was silent. Then, as though she feared that even the walls of her chamber might possess ears with which to hear her secret, she whispered into the ears of Li Nai Ma. Solemnly and fearfully the old nurse began shaking her head, but in her wise eyes was a light of understanding. Beyond all others in the world was she loyal to Eternal Joy.

The first morning of her actual rule came, when Eternal Joy must hold audience for her nobles and issue commands as to the conduct of the duchy's affairs. In accordance with custom, they knelt in the courtyard, while from a dais in the doorway of the palace she looked down upon them.

"Lift up your eyes, friends of my venerated father," she said to them softly. "Well he knew your loyalty, and now his daughter has need of all that loyalty and more. Look upon me and heed my words."

They lifted their heads to affirm their fealty to the new ruler, but their lips closed on the words they would have spoken when their eyes gazed upon Eternal Joy. None in all the Middle Kingdom had ever worn gowns as gorgeous as had always been the gowns of Eternal Joy. But now her gown was as poor as the gown of a tradesman's wife, poorer even than the gown of Li Nai Ma who stood behind the dais. By her gown she might have been the poorest maiden in all Black Dragon Mountain.

"It was known through Black Dragon Mountain," she began, "that Duke Lan Chi was possessed of wealth beyond the wealth of any duke in the Middle Kingdom, is it not true?"

"It is true," they answered with one voice, and shifted on their knees as though they felt ill at ease kneeling in all their glorious ceremonial splendor before a maiden who appeared so suddenly poor and humble. There were servants in the homes of many of the nobles more richly gowned than was Eternal Joy.

"Then I must tell you that it is not true, my loyal retainers!" went on Eternal Joy. "My august father spent with lavish hand and left nothing to me but debts. My gowns have been sold to pay off as many of them as possible. My palace must go to his creditors. I must live on coarse food and have but few servants, perhaps only Li Nai Ma who will always remain faithful. The duchy of Black Dragon Mountain is exceedingly poor because of my father's conduct in affairs of business."

No word came to her from the nobles in answer.

"There is a way, my friends," she went on at last while none noted the visible pounding of her heart. "There must be those among you who wish my hand in marriage. All of you are wealthy, wealthy enough to relieve the duchy of Black Dragon Mountain from the mighty weight of debt. I know that all of you have been more careful than my beloved father, who sits now upon the Dragon Throne and looks down upon us."

"What would you have us do?" the nobles asked.

"Send the matchmakers," she replied, "and him whom I find personable, handsome, and possessed of wealth, will became the husband of Eternal Joy and rule the duchy with her."

"And the duchy is indeed poor?" they asked.

"Poor beyond words to express," she answered.

"But go to your homes now and discuss this matter. When audience is held tomorrow you may send the matchmakers, that I may make my choice from among you."

They made their ceremonial genuflections as they went from the presence of Eternal Joy. After they had gone she caused the doors of the palaces to be closed and locked, disbanded the men-at-arms and dismissed the servants. From the palaces of Duke Lan Chi she went humbly to the home of Li Nai Ma, and caused word to be sent forth that at the home of Li Nai Ma would she hold audience on the following morning. Rich or poor, she still was the ruler of Black Dragon Mountain.

"If only Hu Fo would come," she said in her heart, and even at times she whispered it to Li Nai Ma, who held her peace and did not speak. Li Nai Ma was fearful of this thing they were doing.

"If the nobles talk among themselves, Eternal Joy," she said, "they will wonder who your father's creditors can be, for he owed none of them —and they will know that had there been necessity for him to owe he would first have honored his nobles."

"Each of them will be too occupied with trying to think of excuses to avoid marriage with a poor maiden," said Eternal Joy quietly, "to think of asking questions. For, Li Nai Ma, I have always known that the nobles of Black Dragon Mountain think only of themselves. When morning comes you shall see."

When morning came it brought the nobles, and Eternal Joy smiled to herself when she noted that only the old ones came and those who were already married. She could not have married any one of those who came! Many were the excuses she heard from their lips. This noble had been sent into the mountains on some errand or other and would be away for a long time. This one had received a hurried message from the Throne during the night and had hurried away in the darkness to Peking. That one was desperately ill at home and could not come.

Quickly Eternal Joy made an end of the audience, and the elder nobles escaped with sighs of relief on their lips, many of them stroking beards that were only less indicative of years and wisdom than had been the five-strand beard of Duke Lan Chi.

"You see, Li Nai Ma?" said Eternal Joy when they had gone. "When I am poor there is none to seek my hand in marriage. Had I chosen from among

78

them when they thought me the wealthiest maiden in all the land I should have chosen a man who desired my wealth and power, not a man who loved me. If only Hu Fo—"

But the days came and went and no word came from Hu Fo. It seemed indeed that he would never come, never send her so much as a message of regret that her father had died.

And day by day Eternal Joy seemed poorer, while day by day fewer and fewer nobles came to hold audience with her, so that she ruled the duchy by the words of messengers sent to the home of the nobles. In her hours of need all had deserted her.

"Since they are so plainly lacking in loyalty, Li Nai Ma," said Eternal Joy, "and since none of them wishes me now that I am poor, how could they protest if I wed a man from the people—if one should come?"

"You are thinking of Hu Fo," said Li Nai Ma, "but he does not come and in all propriety you cannot send him a message."

"My heart tells me that he will come," she answered.

Then came a day when not one noble attended the

audience. She knew that they sat in their palatial homes in fear and trembling that somehow they might be called upon to bear some of the burdens of debt the duke had left upon the shoulders of his daughter Eternal Joy. The girl ruler of the duchy smiled to herself, and at Li Nai Ma.

When even the people began to mutter among themselves because their ruler was so poor and had been deserted by the nobles who might have aided her to maintain her court—Hu Fo came.

Once more he came from the east on his great white horse, with the rising sun behind him, turning even his poor garments into gold and covering horse and rider with its brilliance. He came straight to the home of Li Nai Ma, as though he had known where to find Eternal Joy.

He dismounted and dropped to his knees in the dust before the house of Li Nai Ma, while the eyes of Eternal Joy glowed upon him.

"My father is very old, Eternal Joy," he said, "and he could not come himself. There are no matchmakers in the mountains where we live alone, and so none could be sent. I do not come in pity to offer you wealth; because I would not try to buy you and because, however poor, you have that beyond all riches. Your beauty is the beauty of mid-

"This humble person lifts his eyes to the stars."

day without clouds, and of midnight when the moon is clear. Your heart is wealth more precious than money or jewels. Your eyes are more brilliant than the rarest gems. I come then, Eternal Joy, in humble supplication, because I love you more than any words can ever tell you, to ask you to be my bride."

"You wish to rule Black Dragon Mountain with me, Hu Fo?" she asked.

"It is in my heart to wish you were merely a maiden of the people, my beloved," he whispered. "For me there could be no happiness beyond the joy of returning with you to my father to show him the gorgeous beauty of the bride of my choosing. I care not that you are poor, though in return for your vanished riches I give you nothing save love out of the depths of a heart which beats only for you. For power I care less than nothing, save that I would give it back to you who were born to it. I offer nothing but love, ask nothing but love—love more priceless than all the wealth of Black Dragon Mountain and all the combined riches of its disloyal nobles; yes, even than all the gold of the Middle Kingdom, or of the world. This humble person lifts his eyes to the stars."

"Would you have dared tell me this when I was rich?" she whispered.

"I would have told you that first night, because I

knew it then, but for one thing: your wealth. I would never have you think for so much as the space of a heart beat that my love for you was love for your power and your wealth."

Now the soft palms of Eternal Joy gently touched the cheeks of Hu Fo, as she bade him stand to face her. His eyes looked deeply into her eyes, and each knew that a miracle was happening. So for a long time, in the house of Li Nai Ma, they talked together.

But there grew a cloud on the face of Hu Fo, and Eternal Joy insisted on knowing what troubled him.

"No matter what I say," he implored, "you still will love me, still wish me for your bridegroom? For know that always I love you with all my heart."

"No words of yours or mine can change the sweet fact of our love for each other," whispered Eternal Joy, though her whisper was not so low that Li Nai Ma, from an adjoining room, could not hear it by carefully pressing her ear to the panel. "Tell me then this thing which troubles you."

"Beloved Eternal Joy," said Hu Fo, "know then that my father's name is Hu Ling and that before he went to the hills into retirement he was the dearest,

82

most loyal friend of your father. Before you were born he was a noble at the court of Black Dragon Mountain! Since his retirement his wealth has accumulated beyond all his computing and it has been the dream of his heart that his son would one day wed the daughter of Duke Lan Chi; but I wished from the beginning to wed only for love, and so I did not tell you."

"You feared that I would wish you as bridegroom in order that your wealth might rescue me from this poverty into which I have sunk so deeply?" asked Eternal Joy, little fires of anger in her eyes.

"Nay, Eternal Joy," he protested, "I only feared because I loved you so deeply and wished with all my heart that you would love me in return, just for myself. And now that you are poor you know that I love you because you are Eternal Joy, not because you are wealthy and possessed of great power."

The sudden laughter of Eternal Joy was like the music of a mountain stream.

"I too have something to confess," she said at last. "I am not poor. I merely wished my nobles to think me poor. Yet you came, believing me poor, to tell me you loved me because I was Eternal Joy—and now indeed does my name fit me, for joy with you must be eternal. And know, beloved Hu Fo, that even though you were the commoner I believed you, I still would have loved you, still would have wed you."

Now Hu Fo smiled.

"And there is yet something else I must tell you," he said. "Early on the night of the banquet before your father died, he sent a message on rice paper to my father in the mountains, and these were the words of the message: 'Esteemed Hu Ling, aged and venerable friend, my humblest greetings. It is in my heart to hope that you will agree with me—that our children be left themselves to find the way. For how shall we old ones know the way of love between a man and a maiden? They have found each other and they love each other—and there is an old saying that love finds the way for its own delight.'"

"My father was very wise, Hu Fo," Eternal Joy answered—and then unaccountably she laughed again, and when he asked her why she told him.

"I was not thinking of your father or of mine, Hu Fo beloved," she said. "I was dreaming that I saw the faces of all my nobles when word goes out that audience will be held in the morning in the courtyard of the palace of Lan, when they will know that my poverty has been but a jest to test them!"

Hu Fo laughed with her.

"And Hu Fo," she said again, "I shall name the hour of the audience as the hour of sunrise and we shall ride side by side to the palace, with the glory of the sun in our faces."

THE LEGEND OF CHU PAO TAI

THE LEGEND OF CHU PAO TAI

RAGRANT CLOUD, daughter of a mighty official of Hankow, was as happy and joyous as was the sunshiny day on which Chin Yu sent his bridal chair to convey her to his dwelling, where she would abide forever as mistress of his home. Chin Yu was a man of vast substance, and with his marriage to Fragrant Cloud more wealth would accrue to him; for Fragrant Cloud came from a family of untold wealth, whose estates were vast domains upon which countless hundreds of slaves labored to fill to greater repletion the treasury of Fragrant Cloud's father. That father was proud, one of the proudest nobles in His Majesty Chien Lung's Empire. His wealth was so great that he was even sending with Fragrant Cloud in her bridal chair, the *Chu Pao Tai* whose possession had caused in some measure the great good fortune of Fragrant Cloud's father.

Legend told the tale and the tale of the *Chu Pao Tai* was a strange one. The *Chu Pao Tai* was a bag of gold cloth, filled with pearls; and the legend ran that, take howsoever many pearls one might from the bag, it would never be emptied—that for every pearl taken from the *Chu Pao Tai,* a miracle would cause another pearl to appear in its place and the new pearl would be even more perfect than the old.

Of course none believed the legend literally, but that good fortune had attended the family of Fragrant Cloud none could deny—if one knew of the overflowing granaries and the broad fields burdened with rice and millet which Fragrant Cloud had known since childhood. The *Chu Pao Tai,* said the story, had been given to an ancestor of Fragrant Cloud's august father by the Great Sage of Shantung, Confucius himself.

And now, because whatever evil fortune befell him, his wealth could never, he believed, in his lifetime be dissipated; no matter how extravagant he might be, the father of Fragrant Cloud felt he no longer needed to treasure the *Chu Pao Tai.* So, when the bridal sedan chair of Chin Yu came for Fragrant Cloud to bear her to his dwelling place across the mighty river in Wuchang, her father placed as part of her dowry, within the sleeve of her bridal gown, the golden bag, heavily laden with perfectly matched pearls whose value would have ransomed all the slaves of Fragrant Cloud's father. The sleeve of Fragrant Cloud which held the dowry she bore to her husband was very heavy.

The spat spatting of the bare feet of the bridal chair-bearers sounded merrily on the cobblestones as a full two score of them carried the fragile blossom which was Fragrant Cloud to the ferry that would convey her across the sullen Yangtze to Wu-chang. Fragrant Cloud wept, even though she was happy—because it was the custom for a bride to weep upon leaving her father's house and journeying to her husband. It was not considered proper for a maiden to appear happy because she was soon to become a bride. So it was merely because of the custom that Fragrant Cloud wept.

So she came to the ferry and her chair was lowered to the rolling deck by the chair-bearers. There was nothing Fragrant Cloud could see, because she dared not thrust aside the chair-curtains to peer out, lest the eyes of some man other than her husband gaze upon her delicate oval face, so like the blossoms of the peach tree, as lovely and as fragrant with rare perfumes.

But when there came the sounds of other bare feet, the ferry boat trembled slightly and there was a thump on the deck close by, Fragrant Cloud could contain her curiosity no longer. Trembling because of her boldness, she pushed aside the curtains ever so slightly.

Another sedan chair, a bridal chair too, had been lowered to the deck beside hers, so near that she could almost have thrust forth her hand and touched it. But there were only four chair-bearers for the newly arrived chair, by which fact alone Fragrant Cloud knew that the invisible maiden of the other chair was very poor. She was also weeping according to the custom, but, while other brides merely made the sounds of weeping, the invisible bride of the shabby chair was weeping sadly, bitterly, as though some evil fortune were breaking her virgin heart in twain. The heart of Fragrant Cloud was filled with compassion.

She resolved to wait until the coolies had withdrawn into the boat's cabin and then exchange a few words with the unhappy maiden—for her weeping was so sad that it tore at one's heartstrings.

But Fragrant Cloud hesitated, for a sullen darkness had settled over the face of the waters of the mighty Yangtze. From the direction of Wuchang came a threatening roar of sound—and Fragrant Cloud knew instantly that a mighty rain was sweeping across the countryside, a rain whose waters were like a river of the sky in full flood. Against that rain her

Another bridal chair had been lowered to the deck beside hers.

sedan chair would be little protection and its ornate loveliness would be utterly ruined. Not that Fragrant Cloud need mourn the loss of the chair, for to her father and her future husband even the costliest of chairs would be as nothing. Yet how could she leave the chair and show her face to the boatmen and to her own chair-bearers?

The weeping of the bride in the chair beside hers, grew even more heartbreaking as the moments fled and the roaring of the rain swept toward them across the face of the Yangtze. So sorrowful was her weeping that Fragrant Cloud forgot the rain which threatened her and all the gorgeous loveliness of her bridal finery. She thrust the curtain of her chair still further aside to peer out. At that moment the curtains in the other chair were thrust aside and Fragrant Cloud realized that the strange maiden had been looking at her bridal chair since it had been lowered to the deck of the boat. And still the stranger, scarcely less beautiful than Fragrant Cloud herself, continued weeping, until her tears were as plentiful as the vanguard of the rain army which now pattered audibly upon the deck of the boat.

"What is your honorable name?" asked Fragrant Cloud softly.

With a gasp of terror the stranger lowered her

curtain and for many moments remained invisible, though from within her chair came still the sad sound of her weeping. But at last, curiosity overcoming her shyness, the stranger looked forth again.

And now, because the rain fell so heavily and dripped in silver sheets from the roofs of the bridal chairs, the two could scarcely see each other's faces through the downpour.

"What is your honorable name?" Fragrant Cloud repeated her question.

"My humble name, exalted lady, is Moonbeam!" replied the stranger.

"It is a name so beautiful that one wonders why you should weep for sorrow. Do you fear your future husband? What is your sorrow? Why not tell me? We may never meet again so if we tell each other secrets that should not be told we can lock them in our hearts forever. Why, then, are you weeping?"

"It is because, exalted lady, I am so poor and my future husband is so poor. My family has always been poor, and even this despicable bridal chair cost my future husband many times what he could really afford, and I scarcely know whence the money will come with which to pay my chair-bearers. I have always pined for riches and honor for my husband, but I shall never be wealthy and my husband will remain forever poor—because that is the lot of our two families since time began. I weep because I am unhappy in my lot. I dream of lovely things when I sleep—of a vast courtyard in which there are dreaming ponds where goldfish drowse in the sun and come up with wide eyes staring to take their food from my hands. I dream of sedan chairs of gold, of countless servants to obey my slightest wish, of palaces among the mulberry trees, of gorgeous birds in cages to sing to me their love songs throughout the joyous days. But always I waken to find poverty still my burden and the world filled with unhappiness as when I went to sleep."

"Happiness, Moonbeam," said Fragrant Cloud, "rests not in the world's riches but in the human heart. One might possess the gold and silver of all the Universe and yet be utterly unhappy. I am happy, not because I have lived all my life in a palace and have walked always in courtyards where dreamy ponds are crossed by arched bridges of porcelain and goldfish flaunt their jeweled armor in the sun, but because my heart is happy and carefree and I know in my soul that I take happiness, life's one precious jewel, to my husband!"

But the maiden called Moonbeam continued weeping and her tears fell like pearls beside the sedan chair from whose roof the rain fell in sheets, as though the very clouds were weeping too for the sorrow of Moonbeam. As she listened a tender glow came to the heart of Fragrant Cloud and her little hand caressed the bags in her sleeve which were the dowry she bore to her husband. The *Chu Pao Tai* nestled in her hand as though made in the beginning for the clasp of her tiny fingers.

"I have the world," Fragrant Cloud whispered to herself, "and Moonbeam has nothing but sorrow. My father has wealth beyond imagining. There is none in all the Middle Kingdom as wealthy as my honorable father save only Chin Yu, whose wealth must be as great, or even greater perhaps. No one really knows, not even my father—not even Chin Yu himself. What then is this bag of pearls to either my father or my husband?"

Forgetting that the rain was dampening her gorgeous headdress of kingfisher feathers and jewels, Fragrant Cloud leaned the further from the window of her chair, extending to Moonbeam a yellow bag—the *Chu Pao Tai*.

"I have so much and you so little, Moonbeam," said Fragrant Cloud with all compassion, "that the possession of this bag of pearls means less than nothing to me, yet may mean all the world's good fortune

96

to you. Take it, Moonbeam. I give it freely and with a sympathetic heart. It is yours. It was given to my father's honorable ancestor by Confucius, and whoso possesses it is fortunate beyond all dreams of good fortune. There is a tale about the *Chu Pao Tai,* as this bag is called, and the tale is that the bag, however one may try to empty it by removing the pearls, yet remains forever full. It is not entirely true, for often I have counted the pearls, removed two or three from the bag, and counted them again; and always there were less pearls in the bag by exactly the number I had taken. Yet since first this bag was presented to my father's honorable ancestor by the Great Sage, good fortune has attended my father's house—and with this bag go my wishes that good fortune also attend your house hereafter, Moonbeam, and that all your dreams may come true. I ask but one thing: that my name be left on the bag—see, this character is my name character, which means Fragrant Cloud—so that you will remember me, always!"

The boat was by now almost across the mighty river, and the walls and rooftops of Wuchang were visible through the flood of rain ahead. There would be servants there to meet both chairs, and expectantly both maidens lowered their curtains. Neither noticed that the rain had soaked their sedan chairs through, ruined their bridal gowns and that the water in the bottom of the chairs rose even to the tops of their lily-small shoes. For Fragrant Cloud was happy—though she still wept in accordance with custom—that she had been able, by giving so little, to dispel the sorrow in the heart of Moonbeam. And Moonbeam was happy because she had opened the golden bag and peered within to see the many pearls inside, which looked back at her as though they had been countless tiny eyes that smiled upon her. She was happy, so happy that she even wept the more—and her chair-bearers smiled at one another, because their mistress so faithfully followed the custom of weeping on the way to the house of her husband. They would whisper in the ears of their master that his new wife must be dutiful, because she adhered so closely to the aged and honorable conventions.

And so Moonbeam came to the house of her husband Fu Lu, bearing an unexpected dowry in the golden bag of pearls, the *Chu Pao Tai* of Fragrant Cloud, whose face and form she had already forgotten, because she had scarcely noted its contours or its exquisite sweetness through the sheets of rain. For long Moonbeam lived in fear that good fortune would go from the house of her husband, or that there might be some mistake and that Fragrant Cloud would come again for the golden bag of pearls. Only one thing she remembered of what Fragrant Cloud had told her—and on the bag of gold cloth, etched in red, remained the character which was the name character of Fragrant Cloud.

But as the years passed Moonbeam forgot even that, or why the character was not removed. It had become almost a legend in the house of Fu Lu.

Another thing did Moonbeam remember—that the *Chu Pao Tai* brought good fortune to its possessor and that not even the most lavish hand could ever empty it. Yet she recalled that Fragrant Cloud had removed the pearls sometimes and counted them—and that the legend was not literally true. So Moonbeam and her husband hoarded the pearls and never touched them. They believed that the *Chu Pao Tai* brought good fortune—but only if its possessor sought good fortune with his hands and the shrewdness of his brain.

During the years that followed the marriage of Moonbeam to Fu Lu, when Fragrant Cloud had long since been forgotten, many things happened in the Middle Kingdom. To Moonbeam and Fu Lu the most important was the birth of a son, whom they called Chia Lang. To his parents Chia Lang was the greatest son in all the length and breadth of China. Other things happened, too. There were uprisings and unrest throughout the Empire. Ordinary men became great and acquired wealth, became great and important officials, while men who had been great were cast down, their estates confiscated and turned into ruins—and poverty became the portion of men who for generations had known nothing but wealth beyond dreams. Men who had lived in hovels, lived now in the palaces of the mighty ones, who crept into the hovels in their stead.

And always Moonbeam and Fu Lu prospered. They acquired wealth such as neither had ever dared dream of. Fu Lu became Governor of Wuchang and his friends even whispered that one day the Throne would send him abroad as a foreign minister. Moonbeam became hard and avaricious. When she went abroad the poor people made way for her as though she had been the Empress. Her head was held so high that she never saw the common folk who dared cross her pathway, and her own servants were as dust under her exalted feet. She never smiled, save when she thought of Chia Lang and held speech with him— and always she nagged at her husband, bidding him go forth and seek more wealth to add to the uncountable wealth which they already possessed. And always Fu Lu smiled at her and went forth to do her bidding.

THE LEGEND OF CHU PAO TAI

Moonbeam, through the passing years, became so shrewish that she had but two things that she worshiped: her son, Chia Lang, and the *Chu Pao Tai*. The gold cloth bag still held the pearls it had held in the beginning, though Fu Lu could have purchased a whole roomful of bags just like it, each filled with pearls as rich and carefully matched in shape, size, and loveliness. On the second floor of their gorgeous dwelling, that floor which in other houses was usually set aside as a shrine where incense was burned to the gods, or used as a place to store the family's ancestral tablets, was a shrine indeed. But no image of Buddha or of Confucius held the center of the shrine, atop the pedestal of worship. In place of a smiling image, or a frowning image, of Buddha, there rested on the pedestal of sandalwood—the *Chu Pao Tai!* And every day, three times a day, Moonbeam climbed with her husband Fu Lu to the second floor where, with their adored son Chia Lang between them, they kowtowed reverently to the *Chu Pao Tai* which they revered as they had never revered Buddha or the tablets of their honorable ancestors.

And so the years passed until Chia Lang was fifteen years of age and the hopes of Moonbeam and Fu Lu were high for him. He should go to Pei Ching to take the examinations and become a great official like his father. There was nothing this clever son of Moon-beam and Fu Lu might not do. He might even, in these troublous times, when the great were being cast down and the lowly raised up, become China's Emperor. His parents even prayed silently to *Chu Pao Tai* for this wild dream of theirs to come true.

In the sixteenth year of the life of Chia Lang, a ragged, sorrowful woman and her daughter presented themselves at the gate of Fu Lu's outer courtyard. The woman's face had once, perhaps, been beautiful. But now it was wrinkled with care and old with sadness. But her daughter held her head high with pride, though she was as ragged, almost, as was her mother.

"What do you want, bundles-of-old-rags?" demanded the servants of Fu Lu of the old woman and her daughter.

"We are poor and hungry," said the ragged woman, "and we seek but the leavings of rice from the table of your exalted master!"

The servants stared rudely at the woman and even more rudely, with eyes that were waxing bold, at the woman's daughter.

"What is your daughter's name, bundle-of-rags?" the servants asked of the woman.

"Her name is Precious Pearl," said the woman before her daughter could prevent her speaking.

The servants laughed long and boisterously while the faces of mother and daughter reddened with shame.

"Precious Pearl!" they cried. "Precious Pearl! What a sweet name for a bundle-of-rags! Precious Pearl! Do you carry your wealth in your sleeves, Precious Pearl? But of course you do not, because you have no sleeves! Precious Pearl!"

So loudly did the coolies laugh that Chia Lang, dreaming in the garden, heard them and came to find the reason for their mirth. He looked at the woman and her daughter and his heart was filled with compassion.

"My mother," he said to the old woman gently, "needs a new *amah* and a little maidservant. You look honest, both of you, and I shall speak to her and learn whether she might hire you as her *amah* and your daughter as her maidservant. The work is light, for I see you are not strong."

Chia Lang himself led the two to his mother's presence. Moonbeam looked upon the two with her face twisted in high disdain. The ragged old woman knelt humbly before her but Precious Pearl did not kneel and held her head high with pride. Moonbeam looked at her angrily and would have bidden them both begone but for one circumstance. Fortunately for the two strangers, they had been brought to her by Chia Lang, and to him she could refuse nothing.

So, dismissing them as though they had been nothing, Moonbeam nodded curtly, not to the woman and her daughter but to Chia Lang, and the mother became *amah* to Moonbeam, who already had a score of *amahs*, and Precious Pearl became a maidservant among a score of other maidservants.

But one thing only did Moonbeam say to *Ssu Amah*, or *Amah* Number Four, as the mother was called:

"Your duty will be to make sure that the house is always spotlessly clean throughout, though there is one place you must not enter and that is the shrine on the second floor. That you must never visit."

"Your wish is my pleasure, Exalted One," murmured *Ssu Amah* in reply to the stern command of Moonbeam.

And so, day by day, *Ssu Amah* labored endlessly in the residence of Moonbeam and Fu Lu as unnoticed by either as though she had been a bamboo reed, while Precious Pearl waited on the mistress, yet found many hours of idleness on her hands. She might have aided her mother in keeping the house clean, but her mother would not permit it, and so Precious Pearl had much time for dreaming and reading and she scarcely knew whether she loved more the dreaming or the reading.

But always the garden, in which Chia Lang vanished to spend many hours each day, enchanted her. She might not go there, because Young Master strolled there and dreamed whatever dreams Young Masters were wont to dream. Always Precious Pearl, who was fifteen years of age, wondered what she might find in that garden if only she dared enter it. She pictured herself within its secluded walls so often that it was almost as though she were actually there. There would be rockeries, pagodas in the corners and goldfish ponds over which one might lazily pass on high-arched gorgeous bridges. So often did she fancy herself within the garden that she was scarcely surprised when one day, after she had been for three years in the house of Fu Lu, her feet, in spite of all Precious Pearl could do, took her into the garden.

It seemed deserted and, after a few moments of fear, in which she visioned all sorts of punishment that might be hers for trespassing, it seemed almost as though the garden belonged at last to her. Under the trees, among the shadows, peach blossoms had fallen in little pink clouds, and Precious Pearl, who had long since discarded her rags, sat gracefully down among the blossoms which matched to perfection the blossoms painted by Nature in her oval cheeks. Their delicate fragrance stole over her, soothing her, causing her dreams to possess new substance. There were the ponds in which goldfish swam like gold-and-silver arrows, the pagodas in the corners of the walls, the shady seats, the bridges. There were the artificial rocks, pierced by shaded tunnels, the incense burners of brass, the urns of porcelain and silver.

There Precious Pearl opened her book, one that she particularly loved, and began to read—while the perfume of rich flowers charmed her—and her world of dreams became, for the time, a world that was real at last.

"You are like a beautiful blossom in my garden, Precious Pearl," said a laughing voice beside her.

Precious Pearl leaped to her feet to face Young Master, and her cheeks mantled with shame at being discovered. She looked this way and that, seeking a way of escape, though Young Master did not appear to be angry in the least. She put her book behind her and swayed back and forth on her feet, hoping to hide from Chia Lang the fact that her knees were visibly trembling through her gown.

"Oh, Young Master," said Precious Pearl, finding her voice at last, "I did not think anyone was here, else I would never have dared intrude in your garden. I looked around carefully, yet saw no one. I am sorry. May I have your permission to go now, Young Master?"

The eyes of Precious Pearl filled with tears of embarrassment, and still she held the book behind her.

"What are you reading?" Chia Lang demanded, though his voice was not as stern as he pretended.

"It . . . it . . . is just . . . a . . . a . . . book," said Precious Pearl. "It could not possibly interest any but a humble person of such mean station as myself! It could not interest one so exalted as Young Master!"

"Let me see it!" said Chia Lang sharply.

Precious Pearl dared not disobey Young Master. Shyly, trembling more than before, she held forth the book. Chia Lang took it and his brows arched with surprise.

"Why, Precious Pearl!" he said at last. "It is one of the most difficult of the Higher Classics! Its language is so difficult that I myself can scarcely read it! Do you really read it, or do you just pretend?"

Precious Pearl flushed again.

"I once had a wonderful tutor, when I was but a small person," she told him, "and I studied very hard. Then we were wealthy. Afterward—when we were no longer wealthy—I studied alone, and I love these poems as I love nothing else."

"Tell me of the time when you were wealthy!" commanded Chia Lang, his face full of interest.

Then Precious Pearl remembered the proprieties.

"It is not proper, Young Master," she said in a low voice, "that I, a humble maidservant, remain here in the garden in converse with you. For Confucius says that after the age of seven years a boy and a girl should not even sit at table together!"

The interest deepened in the face of Chia Lang.

"How does it happen," he said, "that you, the daughter of an ordinary servant, know the proprieties and are able to speak with the words of the Great Sage?"

"I should never speak of these things," said Precious Pearl in a low voice, "with a Young Master as wonderful as your exalted self. My mother has forbidden me ever to speak of these things; but there are things I remember, about which I have not spoken to her, and about which, therefore, she has never forbidden me to speak. I remember, when I was a small person, there was a garden like this one, with goldfish ponds and pagodas, rockeries and arched bridges. Countless servants did my bidding; ornate sedan chairs carried me, and there were many rich things. I was in that garden, with an *amah*, dreaming in the brilliant sunlight or sleeping in the shade of peach and mulberry trees—"

She broke off suddenly, again remembering, and this time Young Master did not detain her as she fled from the garden as though pursued by a dragon. But he called after her softly:

"Come to my garden tomorrow and the tomorrow after that if you wish and all the other tomorrows after that one—and none shall forbid you!"

Though Precious Pearl heard the words of Young Master she did not look back, but next day she came to the garden again and this time she talked longer with Young Master.

The days passed swiftly and happily. The sun never shone brighter; the goldfish were never more resplendent in their shining mail of gold and silver; and the world was, of all worlds, the very best in which to live. Chia Lang said so, and Precious Pearl said so, but neither admitted that this was so because they loved each other. Chia Lang did not know it, did not even guess—until one day a prying servant carried a tale to Moonbeam, who was growing old and fat and more avaricious than ever.

Angry and a little afraid, she sent for her beloved son Chia Lang.

"You have been meeting Precious Pearl in the garden!" she snapped at Chia Lang.

"Yes," he admitted readily, "I have, august mother. But there has been no harm, and she is a daughter of a once excellent family. The uprisings caused the death of her father and the loss of his estates; and this is true, because she knows the Higher Classics and the Book of Changes and quotes the poems of Li Po as well as I!"

"So you have been talking poetry with each other!" snapped Moonbeam, who, if she had ever heard of Li Po, had forgotten entirely that she had; because she had been too busy nagging her husband to add to his wealth to acquire more of learning than she had possessed that rainy day when she had crossed the mighty Yangtze to become the bride of Fu Lu.

"She is of good family," said Chia Lang stoutly, "even though she is poor and the daughter of an *amah!*"

"Do you mean that you have been making speeches of love to each other?" demanded Moonbeam. "I shall inform your father immediately and he will see that you go at once to Pei Ching to take your examinations and to forget your foolishness."

But Chia Lang looked so crestfallen that Moonbeam relented, at least enough to smile at him with a trace of pity on her sagging cheeks—for she worshiped her son and there was nothing she could deny him.

"After all, my beloved son," she said more softly, "she *is* the daughter of a woman who has been for years an *amah* in the household of which you are Young Master. Nothing changes that. You could never marry her, because it is not the custom for one of your exalted station to marry one so poor. Both came to the gate in rags and they will leave in rags if ever the time comes when I dismiss them."

"Please do not dismiss them!" cried Chia Lang. "I love her, my august mother! I knew it not 'til now, but I love her and wish her to be my bride!"

Moonbeam closed her lips tightly and waved her son away and on her face was an expression which told Chia Lang that she believed utter woe had fallen at last upon the house of Fu Lu.

Chia Lang went straight away to the garden where he knew he would find Precious Pearl. He did find her there and she was bitterly weeping. He took her in his arms for the first time and she did not try to prevent him. Perhaps she wished to be in his arms. Perhaps her sorrow was so deep that she did not realize. But he opened his arms and she stepped into them and wept against his shoulder, so that her tears fell like pearls down the front of his rich robe.

"The servants," she moaned. "They have told my

111

mother and she says that we must go immediately! She says only trouble can come of love between Young Master and the daughter of an *amah*. So she makes plans to leave! After three years we depart—in rags as we came—and I must leave you forever, oh, my beloved!"

There was nothing he could say. There were the customs which might not be denied. Nothing could change them, not even death.

"And I, too, must go," he whispered, "for my august mother also knows the truth, and I must go away— away to Pei Ching, to take my examinations. I shall become an official and go perhaps to another province to become governor and we never again may see each other!"

And before Chia Lang realized it his tears were flowing, too, and mingling with the tears of Precious Pearl.

That night there was much weeping in the home of Fu Lu. Chia Lang was yet a boy, and he wept because he could never have Precious Pearl to be his bride. Precious Pearl wept for the same reason. *Ssu Amah* wept with abject sorrow because once this marriage, which now could never transpire, would have been the finest in all the Empire—when her husband had been great in the land, second to none in wealth.

"My Precious Pearl," she moaned, "we must go. Poverty must again be our portion."

And then she could not go on—for she was remembering many things, little things, whispers she had heard among the servants during the years she had been in the house of Fu Lu, years during which she had never once entered the rooms on the second floor, where, the servants whispered, the master and mistress worshiped, not Buddha or the gods of the household, but a bag of gold.

"Surely," *Ssu Amah* told herself, "when they have so much and we have so little they will never miss it from their boundless store."

For she had also heard that the bag was never opened, but merely worshiped. She could put other things in place of gold and bear the gold away. It was stealing, but it was for Precious Pearl. Some day there would be another who would love her, and she should have a dowry to take to that one. If *Ssu Amah* was caught, she would be severely punished, might even lose her life—but Precious Pearl need never know.

When Precious Pearl had fallen asleep still weeping, so that tears crept forth from under her black lashes, *Ssu Amah* rose from her bed and, softly, gently, climbed to the secret room on the second floor. She bore a candle which she would light when she had entered the room and closed the door.

But there was still another person in the house who wept and whispered to herself as she wept—Moonbeam!

"Oh, oh," she moaned. "All the wealth I have wished for is ours. Yet my son, whom above all others I love, is unhappy. If we were poor again, as we once were, he might wed this daughter of an *amah* and be happy, because he would never know differently. Now, he has always had riches and could not live without them. I could not rob him of them if I would —yet I must rob him of something just as precious to him. Oh, woe is my portion, because Chia Lang weeps and will not be comforted! But he may not wed Precious Pearl, else every official in the land will ridicule him and laugh at him and he will be compelled to hide his head in shame! Oh, woe is my portion! I would rather live in rags than that Chia Lang have one moment of unhappiness! And it is all because of the *Chu Pao Tai!* I wish I had never seen it!"

So a kind of fury possessed the heart of Moonbeam as she quitted her bed. She thought of destroying the golden bag, now dim with the passing years. She thought of offering up prayers for some miracle that would still allow Chia Lang to be great and yet possess Precious Pearl as his wife. She scarcely knew what she wished, but she connected her sorrows as always she had connected her joys, with the *Chu Pao Tai*—which she now went forth to see again. Perhaps in the silence of the family shrine she might think of a way.

She entered the room and started back—for there, standing before the pedestal, clasping the *Chu Pao Tai* to her breast, while her tears fell like rain, was *Ssu Amah!*

Moonbeam caught her murmured words.

"Mine! Mine! It belonged to my father and now it is mine—and nothing can ever take it from me again. She does not need it—and I gave it to her when she did. Now I need it and she must give it to me. No! No! I cannot, even for Precious Pearl—for I gave it freely—"

Ssu Amah slowly extended her hands to return the *Chu Pao Tai* to its pedestal.

Moonbeam stood as one turned to stone staring at the wrinkled, tear-stained cheeks of her *amah*. Finally, she extended her hand, and a forefinger, pointing.

"Yours?" she asked hoarsely. "Yours? Tell me! Why do you say it is yours?"

"Because it was mine. I knew your name was Moonbeam, but I could not be sure, for there are many ladies called Moonbeam in the Middle Kingdom."

"Speak!" interrupted Moonbeam. "A lady of high degree gave me that bag of pearls! Speak and tell me her name, for only one other person now living would know that lady's name."

"Her name, mistress," *Ssu Amah* clutched the *Chu Pao Tai* the tighter to her breast as she softly spoke, while her eyes were wide and seemed to be looking far, far back into the past, "her name was Fragrant Cloud!"

"More proof still!" insisted Moonbeam, hoarsely, so that her voice was like a file. "I must know more."

"Our bridal chairs," whispered *Ssu Amah*, "were side by side on the Hankow bank of the great river and it was raining. I wept because I was happy, you wept because you were poor."

Now a smile that transfigured her face spread outward from the lips of Moonbeam and she trembled as though she was very tired and could find no place to rest.

She held out her arms to *Ssu Amah*, who once had been Fragrant Cloud, and the two mothers wept together—and laughed through their tears. And the *Chu Pao Tai* which had once belonged to Fragrant Cloud was hers again, because Moonbeam had given it to her.

116

"It will buy the most gorgeous bridal gown in China," said Moonbeam, "and one would scarce miss one of the pearls one sold to buy it. It will buy a grand house and many clothes of great richness—and when Precious Pearl comes in the bridal chair Chia Lang shall send for her, she will be so changed that the servants will never recognize her. So go, Fragrant Cloud, and take your daughter with you! You are dismissed forever from the household of Fu Lu—as *amah!* But make ready the bridal gown and prepare your daughter to receive the bridal chair of my son when it comes to the house you must buy—with pearls of good fortune from the *Chu Pao Tai!*"

"But," murmured Fragrant Cloud, "should we tell—"

"Yes," replied Moonbeam, "let us send for Fu Lu. Let us send for Chia Lang, and for Precious Pearl! Let us gather here in the shrine of *Chu Pao Tai,* which now becomes a shrine indeed, and weep together and tell each other the glad tidings! For to-morrow, when I dismiss you and Precious Pearl from our home, I wish to know that, behind your apparent sadness as you go, you are smiling, because you know that you will return again—and that the sun will shine upon us all, forever!"

AT THE GATE OF KWAN YIN

AT THE GATE OF KWAN YIN

N the heart of Hangchow, on the shores of beautiful, somnolent Lake Hsi Hu, was an ancient Chinese dwelling which had belonged to one family of illustrious ancestry for forgotten generations. The last master of this home had ascended the Dragon Throne on High many moons past and had left his widow, Huang Mu, to guard their rarest treasure, the lovely Mei Mei of seventeen summers.

Huang Mu had cared zealously for this young daughter of the smiling face and innocent eyes. Mei Mei had learned all the rules of filial piety; she had studied the Classics; she knew and respected the ancient customs; but—she knew nothing of men.

Long years before her father had gone to join his illustrious ancestors, he had betrothed Mei Mei—as was the custom—to Pao Bei, the son of one of his friends. That had been when Mei Mei and Pao Bei were mere children and Mei Mei only slightly remembered her betrothed as a lad with large eyes and smiling lips.

Soon now it would be time for Pao Bei's matchmaker to come to make arrangements for their wedding. As the time drew near, Huang Mu, the wise mother, instructed Mei Mei in the dutiful love of faithful wife for good husband.

Mei Mei wondered if Pao Bei had changed greatly from the lad who long ago had come calling with his father. She had liked him then, would she like him now? She never really doubted it, for a maiden naturally loved the man an illustrious father chose. She would be a faithful, virtuous wife to Pao Bei, and they would go through life together, hand-in-hand to the very grave.

And when the wedding time came, Pao Bei would be proud of her. In all Hangchow no maiden possessed such gorgeous robes as those of Mei Mei. And sometimes she told herself shyly that no maiden so matched the beauty of her garments as did Mei Mei. There was one special gown at which she loved to gaze, touching it here and there with her small and shapely fingers. It was jade green, as though a bit of the gorgeous waters of Hsi Hu had been turned into silk and fashioned into a gown for the time when the bridal chair of Pao Bei would come for Mei Mei.

Thinking of the time when she must leave forever the home of Huang Mu brought sadness to Mei Mei's heart, but her mother comforted her.

AT THE GATE OF KWAN YIN

"Daughters must always go to the homes of their husbands, as I went to the home of your father when he sent the bridal chair. It is inevitable, and though I shall sorrow for the loss of your glad presence here, I shall be happy in the fact that you have a good and honest husband—to whom you will be a virtuous wife, and to whom you will give many children to comfort you and Pao Bei when you are old in your turn."

It was of these words of her mother's that Mei Mei thought as she sat in the summerhouse in the center of the courtyard and gazed out across the broad green bosom of Hsi Hu. Her eyes rested idly upon the island with a gorgeous pagoda where people went in beautiful house boats to make merry.

"I must go," she told herself, "to the Goddess of Mercy Temple to worship—to pray that all my life —though I live to be very old, I shall be a faithful, worthy wife to Pao Bei."

She sent Little Bamboo, her maid, to order her sedan chair with its liveried bearers. Mei Mei told her mother that she would like to go to the temple to pray that she be made worthy of the love of Pao Bei. Huang Mu nodded permission and returned softly to her own chambers. Mei Mei stepped into her chair, dropped the curtains to hide her beauty from the eyes of the curious, and bade her bearers transport her to the temple by the way that led past the tombs of her father and his illustrious ancestors.

How well she knew that solemn enclosure where her father's people slept. There the limbs of the trees inside the great wall seemed to bend a little lower as though to protect the mounds from the sun and the rains. There the birds seemed to twitter more softly as though they knew they sang in a place that was holy. There was the tablet of gorgeous white jade bearing some inscriptions that were new, and some that were very old indeed—telling of the deeds of her people who had gone.

Mei Mei parted the curtains of her chair as she was borne past the tombs to the spat-spat of bearers' feet on the curving road that led back from Hsi Hu to the Goddess of Mercy Temple, just beyond the tombs. When she returned she would pause for a moment to enter the sacred place and read again the inscriptions which spoke of the good deeds of her family. These she must not forget—they would make her a more worthy bride.

But now she went on, and shortly was set down before the temple gate by her bearers. They might not enter here, for the temple was for women and was served by nuns. Mei Mei loved the nuns because they were kind to her always and told her marvelous

Kwan Yin—Goddess of Mercy

stories. For a moment she thought of herself as one of them—with all her raven-black hair gone forever—with little black spots burned on the crown of her head to indicate she had taken her vows—and with the doors of the outer world closed against her forever. She shuddered. But of course that would never happen to her!

Mei Mei entered the temple grounds, and her bearers—knowing her custom of spending much time there with the nuns—went away for a while, to return later when they thought she would be ready to depart. But this time—because she planned to visit her father's tomb on her way home—Mei Mei did not remain after she had prayed to Kwan Yin for guidance. So when she was ready to depart, her bearers were nowhere to be found. However, the ground about the temple was avoided by men, so Mei Mei would be violating none of the proprieties by walking unattended the short distance to the tombs. She would go there and await her bearers.

She entered the grounds through the gate that was always open so that wayfarers might enter, rest for a while in peace, and gain in piety by reading the inscriptions on the tablet of white jade. This tablet was on a pedestal at the top of nine short steps, and was covered by a summerhouse to keep the sun and rains from marring the still white beauty of the jade. Mei Mei strolled quietly among the tombs, and over all the quiet enclosure the voices of her people seemed to whisper.

As she reveled in the quiet and peace she did not realize that the clouds had darkened the sun, and that the rain was coming down. When she discovered this the bearers still were absent. They would expect her to remain in the temple while the rain lasted, and would not come until it was over. So she must find shelter, and the summerhouse which covered the white jade tablet was very near. She hurried to enter the summerhouse where the rain could not reach her, and sat on the lowest of the nine clean steps.

Scarcely had Mei Mei left her home on the shore of Hsi Hu than the matchmaker of Pao Bei's father had come to ask of her mother when the bridal chair should be sent; and while she rested in the summer-house, waiting for the rain to pass that now murmured gently on the tiles above her head, her mother and the matchmaker were perusing the book of good and evil portent, to decide upon an auspicious day for Mei Mei to go in the bridal chair of Pao Bei.

As she sat there a sound came from beyond the jade tablet which towered above her head. She stiffened, for she felt that she was not alone in the summerhouse.

Someone else was just beyond the towering white tablet.

"Who is there?" she asked softly, when the sound did not come again.

Around the tablet came a handsome young man, whose gown proved him wealthy and of excellent family. Mei Mei regarded him in some confusion.

"I am very sorry," he said softly, and she thought as he spoke that his voice sounded strangely like the small waves that broke along the shores of Hsi Hu in the calmness of summer, "but there seemed to be no one here, and so I entered to await the passing of the storm. I must go now, for it is wrong for me to speak with you alone. It would mean disgrace for you if anyone knew."

Mei Mei's heart was beating faster with a strange eagerness. Something in the eyes of this young man seemed to speak to her, before he cast them down discreetly.

"But if your servants are here—" she began.

"I sent them on," he told her, "to find shelter for themselves when I knew that the rain was coming. And now I must follow them."

"You are welcome to remain," she said softly. "There can be no harm, and the storm is heavier. I bid you welcome here."

"You bid me welcome? Then this is—"

"The tomb of my ancestors. Here my father lies among his people."

"But if someone came—" he hesitated.

"None will come now, because it rains," she answered him, "and there can be no harm, because we shall never meet again."

He sat down quietly beside her, but well apart, and smiled at her—and in his smile she once more saw a hint of Hsi Hu, which to her was a symbol of all that was lovely and right and good. He was very handsome. His hands were shapely, and his gown was of great richness.

"Are you betrothed?" He still was hesitant.

"I am betrothed to Pao Bei," she answered. "I was betrothed in childhood."

"Then in truth it is wrong for me to speak with you!" He rose to go, but still she detained him.

"There is no wrong, my people whisper in my heart," she told him, "and for a little while let us hold speech together. Tell me who you are, whence you come, and what transpires in the great world beyond the hills of Hangchow."

"My name is Yu Ting," he told her, "and since we may never meet again, and even this is forbidden, I must tell you what is in my heart. If I had known

128

that anywhere in Hangchow there resided a maiden as fair as you, I should long since have asked my father to send a matchmaker. But that is impossible now, since you are betrothed. Will you tell me your name?"

"It is Mei Mei." She flushed a little at the words he had spoken. "I live with my mother on the shores of Hsi Hu, whence I look out across the jade green waters and dream, and wonder what people do on the island in the lake, because so often I hear the joy in their laughter."

She did not feel that Yu Ting had been bold in telling her that had he known of her he would have sent a matchmaker, for she did not know when a man was bold and when he was not, because she knew nothing at all of men. But this she knew, it must not be wrong if Yu Ting did it, because in her eyes, even so soon after she had met him, he could not do a thing that was bold or wrong. In her eyes he had found greater favor than Mei Mei knew. She wished to linger on and talk further, and listen to the musical words that fell from his lips.

And so they sat on, scarcely realizing how much each told the other, and how much each read in the eyes of the other that neither had spoken in words. But Mei Mei knew that for a time she had forgotten Pao Bei, and knew from the eyes of Yu Ting that he had thought only of her while they talked together.

It was Yu Ting who realized that the storm was over. He rose, and his eyes smiled at her, and his lips.

"Mei Mei," he murmured, " 'Twice Beautiful,' I go now, wishing that I might linger forever with you; and wherever I go the world will be empty without you."

Her delicate face flushed, but she did not rebuke him, because she treasured his words which made her heart beat the faster. All she could say was:

"How do you travel?"

"My horse is outside the wall—and I travel—away!"

She was not to know, then, whither he traveled. Perhaps it was better this way, for the betrothed of Pao Bei must never again think of another.

She walked with him to the gate. She watched him mount, and as he rode away, very straight on his horse like a soldier, she waved to him, not caring at all that the proprieties were offended.

He rode from sight without looking back again— and for the first time she was conscious that two sedan chairs were meeting on the road that led past the tombs. One was her own come to find her. One traveled the opposite direction, and from behind the half raised curtain a face filled with disapproval looked out at her. It was the face of the father of Pao Bei! Then the curtain fell, and the chair went on to the spat-spat of the bearer's feet on the curved way. Mei Mei, not realizing what the chance encounter might mean to her, returned to her mother's house.

Now that the rain was over, Hsi Hu looked more deeply green and lovely, the sun was a disc of gold in the sky, and the birds in the garden sang sweetly— Mei Mei was happy. She was thinking of Yu Ting, who had ridden away, never once looking back after she had waved. She had already forgotten the passing sedan chair of Pao Bei's father.

But she remembered very soon, because the matchmaker for Pao Bei came almost at once—and through the half opened door of her room she heard him hold astounding speech with aged Huang Mu.

"My master bids me tell you," said the matchmaker with all courtesy, "that Pao Bei no longer desires the hand of Mei Mei in marriage! He bids me tell you that Mei Mei has disgraced her family and his. He bids me say that nothing can alter his august decision —since now in all honor there is nothing left for Mei Mei to do, save take her own life! She was seen at the gate of her ancestral tombs, holding speech with a strange man! The tale of this disgrace will travel through all Hangchow; demand will be made that she make full atonement—and the only atonement is self-destruction!"

Aged Huang Mu swayed like a limb that is stricken by the storm as she listened to the matchmaker's words. Mei Mei's heart almost stopped beating with terror, while her feet refused to take her from her room, so that she might tell this matchmaker she was guilty of no wrong. Yet—

She remembered, and did not go. The matchmaker was right, according to the ancient virtues. She had talked alone with a man, and had indeed disgraced her father who was gone, and all his ancestors before him.

But when the matchmaker, with many genuflections, had taken his departure, and the house had fallen awesomely silent—Mei Mei came forth bravely, with her head held high.

"I did speak with a man among the tombs, little mother," she whispered. "But there was no wrong. I feel here in my heart, which flutters so, that I did no wrong. According to august custom Pao Bei is right. But I need not slay myself. I can remain with you forever."

"But if nothing is done to atone—" said trembling old Huang Mu.

And silence hung between them while the mind of

Mei Mei was busy with thought. Then she raised her head to tell her mother all that had occurred.

"There is indeed no wrong," her mother told her. "But if no atonement is made—and Pao Bei tells why he does not send the bridal chair—all Hangchow will believe that there was something wrong."

"I shall make atonement," said Mei Mei softly, "and Hangchow shall know that I am accused unjustly. I shall be near you, little mother—for I shall join the sisters who serve Kwan Yin, in the Goddess of Mercy's Temple."

"Think well, my Mei Mei, for to become one with the sisters there you must forsake the world, its riches, its beauties—and once your vows are taken, never may you be wife to any man."

Proudly Mei Mei raised her head.

"I shall have with me always the memory of Yu Ting, and that he was most kind."

Next morning, heart heavy with sadness at parting, Mei Mei went from room to room of her home —bidding each spot good-by. She touched with caressing fingertips the little things she had known since she could remember; she traced the embroidered beauties in the tapestries on the walls of her sleeping place; she looked at the tables and chairs which were old and on the pictures of her father's people who slept the long sleep in the tombs where disaster had found and claimed her. Behind her as she made her journey of farewell, there followed on shuffling feet Little Bamboo, her maid who had held her on ample knees and carried her on broad hips when she had been a baby. And Little Bamboo was weeping.

"I bid good-by to you too, Little Bamboo," whispered Mei Mei. "For I shall not need you while I serve Kwan Yin."

"But I shall serve you always, little mistress," wept Little Bamboo. "I too shall go to worship Kwan Yin —and cut off my hair, and burn the black spots on my head when I take the vows with you, so that we shall always be together, because I love you!"

"Think well," whispered her mother at parting, "before the final vows are taken. Many moons will pass at the temple before you take them, so that you shall have time to decide—"

"I have already decided, little mother; but I will think well upon the matter while I am being prepared for my vows."

"I shall come to you every day, Mei Mei," said Huang Mu. "And on the day you take your vows I shall visit you, and ask you if you are sure you wish to take them."

"And then, as now," said Mei Mei bravely, "I shall

know that the vows must be taken."

And so she went to the Goddess of Mercy Temple, and Huang Mu remained at home with the servants —save only Little Bamboo, who had gone to the temple with her mistress, to take the vows with her when the time came, many moons hence.

As the matchmaker had said, Pao Bei's father spread the story through Hangchow, so that all his friends, and enemies—especially the enemies who might laugh at him—might know why he did not send the bridal chair for Mei Mei, to bring her to his home as the wife of Pao Bei. All Hangchow agreed that Mei Mei had disgraced her family; but all Hangchow agreed too, after the whole tale had been told, that Mei Mei was making full atonement. Surely, they said, she could not be guilty of any wrong, else she would not have gone to the temple—to have her head shaved, and the black spots burned on her crown. For the days and weeks passed, and the moons, and the temple still held her—and soon her vows would be taken.

The name that was mentioned most often in Hangchow was the name of Mei Mei; the tale that was told most frequently was the tale of her atonement; and the belief that was strongest in Hangchow was the belief in her innocence.

Word of what had happened even went out of Hangchow, and over the mountains which surrounded it—mountains which held in their heart the jewel that was jade green Hsi Hu—and was heard at last by Yu Ting.

He had made inquiries about Mei Mei everywhere in Hangchow; but because all knew she was the betrothed of Pao Bei none would tell him where she lived.

When Yu Ting heard the news, he told his story, too.

"There was no wrong," he told his listeners. "We only talked together. Had she not been betrothed I should have asked my father to send the matchmaker, for in all the Middle Kingdom there is no maiden more lovely, more wondrous, shy, and desirable. All that has befallen her is a fault that must be charged to me, and it is I who should make the atonement demanded of her. But how shall I find her?"

"She has entered the Goddess of Mercy Temple, where she will soon take her vows," they told Yu Ting, "and you may not see her, for men are forbidden the temple, and the nuns there will guard her zealously."

But the face of Yu Ting, which was a fine face because his heart was good, and his soul was honest—became very grave. He spoke no word of his plans to

136

his friends—and of these there were many because, not only was the family of Yu Ting great, but he was loved for his own sake. He left his father's house, behind the mountains called Hu Shan which surrounded Hangchow, and rode his strongest horse toward the province. He scarcely knew what he would do, but knew he must do something.

"She must never, never think that I come to her in pity," he told himself as he rode. "I am glad beyond words that even among the tombs where we first met I told her what was in my heart—that if she were not already betrothed I would ask my father to send the matchmaker."

On the very day that Mei Mei was to take her vows, Yu Ting came to the gate which led into the temple grounds. Huang Mu was with her child to make sure that Mei Mei did not mistake the wishes of her own heart. But Yu Ting was stopped at the gate by an aged nun, who was ugly, and shabbily dressed, whose hair was shaved off, and whose crown was burned with the black spots which proved that long ago she had taken her vows.

"Young stranger," said the old nun with asperity, "what do you wish here? Do you know that no man may enter these grounds? Do you not know that within is the temple of the Goddess of Mercy, where only women may come to worship?"

"I have come far, holy woman," he told her humbly, dismounting to bow his head, "and I would worship at the shrine."

"It is forbidden to men," she answered harshly. "Therefore mount and ride away!"

In desperation then he told her many things. He told her of what had transpired at the tombs, of the moons of waiting, and hoping, and of how at last he had come, seeking news of Mei Mei—whose name meant Twice Beautiful.

Grimly the aged woman stepped aside.

"From where you stand you may see her," she said. "She kneels before the goddess to pray."

Yu Ting, with heavy heart, peered past the old nun, across the drab courtyard and through the door of the temple itself. There he could plainly see her—his heart's desire—his Mei Mei. She knelt on the cold stones before a shrine he could not see, and her face was lifted, while all about her knelt the others who had taken the vows before her, down the years which led away into the past. The gorgeous black hair of Mei Mei hung free, and flowed over her shoulders and below her waist like a mantle. Her face, even at this distance, was a face transfigured, alight with brave resolve.

138

AT THE GATE OF KWAN YIN

"Note her hair, young stranger," said the ancient woman, whom Yu Ting scarcely heard. "In a few heartbeats this beauty will be taken from her and never again be allowed to grow. She will take her vows, and the crown of her head will be burned with black spots to show that she belongs henceforth and forever to Kwan Yin. See how the sisters kneel and pray with her? They will be happy to welcome her into the shrine, for all of us love her."

"And I love her, too, old one," said Yu Ting, agony in his voice. "I love her! It is because of me that this thing has happened to her, and I have come to make atonement. Let me speak with her, if only for a moment, before the vows are taken."

"You cannot enter. She is praying, and the sisters with her. They must not be disturbed. Again I bid you, young stranger, mount and ride!"

"But is there none who will listen? None who will hearken to my words? I would tell of my love for Mei Mei. She is young, and life for her would be sweet. She should not forsake the world—when she is truly innocent of wrongdoing. I, who am a man, should be the one to atone. Help me, holy one—for my heart is heavy."

"And the time is short," she finished for him. She pondered the matter, while Yu Ting's eyes never left that kneeling figure, and the others that surrounded it, as though Mei Mei herself had been the shrine, and the rest there to worship her and offer up their prayers. "Yes, the time is short. But until her vows have been taken there is but one who may speak for her, in all propriety. That one is her aged mother, Huang Mu, who kneels in the temple with her, praying."

"Send her then, sister," implored Yu Ting.

Shaking her head doubtfully, yet forced on by Yu Ting's insistence, and by something bright and glowing and earnest, that her wise old eyes had seen in his, the aged keeper of the portal turned and left him standing there. All too slowly the nun moved toward the temple doors.

A moment or so of waiting—and each seemed ages long—and then another old one came who was not a nun.

"I am Huang Mu, mother of Mei Mei," said the newcomer simply. "You would speak with me?"

"Yes, little mother. I am Yu Ting. It was I who spoke with Mei Mei among the tombs. It is I who have brought Mei Mei to this. In all honor to Kwan Yin, it is in my heart to say that Mei Mei must not take the vows. I do not come in pity. I do not come as duty bound. I come because, of all things this world possesses for me, Mei Mei is the most precious. Had she not already been betrothed on that day when the rain fell, and trapped us both together among the tombs of her illustrious ancestors, I should have come straight to you and asked to send the matchmaker. Now she is no longer betrothed, though soon she will belong to Kwan Yin—and I have the right to speak. I would ask my father to send the matchmaker, but there is no time. Only go to her, while yet your word is the law which binds her; ask her to come to me here at the gate, and hear my words."

Long and earnestly Huang Mu looked into the eyes of Yu Ting.

His eyes met hers unafraid, and what she saw in them brought to her lips a soft smile that ran gently among the wrinkles on her aged face. Huang Mu turned and moved into the temple. Looking past her, Yu Ting saw that the nuns were rising to their feet, and knew that the time was short indeed.

All eternity passed while feeble Huang Mu moved slowly toward the door—which would close to end all hope for Yu Ting, or remain open to show him heaven, and Mei Mei, if she would come.

Then his heart almost stopped beating, for with her head still held high, and her eyes deep filled with courage, she was coming to him across the courtyard's cobblestones—in answer to the simple words her mother had whispered into her ear.

"There is one, a stranger, who begs a word with you at the gate. In your place I would go to hear his words—before your vows are taken."

Wondering she had listened, had noted the gentle smile on her mother's wrinkled face—and now across the cobblestones she was coming.

Her eyes met the eyes of Yu Ting, and the faces of both were alight with joy.

Out of the temple behind her came the nuns, amazed at what they saw. Near she came, and nearer. The nuns listened, and looked at one another, and wondered why Mei Mei did not speak, and why this young stranger had no words with which to greet her as she came.

Slowly she approached him, while he waited to receive her—because he dared not advance beyond the gate which gave upon the courtyard.

Would these two who met so strangely never speak? They merely advanced, eyes on eyes, lips trembling, while no words came.

Then—

Mei Mei had passed through the gate, as though she had never known it was a gate at all, as though she had forgotten that soon her vows were to be taken,

binding her forever to Kwan Yin, great and good Goddess of Mercy.

Her right hand lifted gently and was clasped in the
hand of Yu Ting, reverently held forth to receive it.

And still no words were spoken.

Once again Yu Ting rode away, this time toward
the sunset, and once again he did not look back—nor
did Mei Mei, whose black hair flowed free, mantling
her shoulders to her waist.

What need for words?

What need to turn again and look behind?

For Yu Ting and for Mei Mei, who rode before him
on the horse which was strong to carry two, all the
world lay ahead.

THE AMBER TALISMAN

THE AMBER TALISMAN

URING the brief nineteen years of his life, Chang Ho had performed, gladly and freely, all the twenty-four acts of filial piety, and was a son in whom his father, Chang Fu Lung, was well pleased. It was the desire of the loyal heart of Chang Fu Lung that his son should follow in his august footsteps and become a great soldier for His Majesty. Chang Fu Lung was old and his shoulders were bowed with the weight of his vast responsibilities. He wished with all his soul that his son should lift those burdens from him so that he might spend the remaining few years of his life in peace and quiet far from the battlefields he had known for so long.

That he should be deserving of his father's faith and confidence was the wish of Chang Ho, and to that end he spent the long summer days in his father's garden where he practised the arts of the soldier. His tight-fitting black garments of the soldier gave full play to his already mighty muscles as he practised endless hours at archery—and it was seldom indeed that his arrows missed the target at which the young man aimed. He was justly proud of his archery, and his father, who came to watch the mighty exploits of his son, was often seen to nod his hoary head with satisfaction.

Chang Ho had carefully, under his father's guidance, mastered all the muscles of his body. He had begun as a mere child, nine years before, by lifting the smallest of the stone lions which his father had ordered carved and placed on pedestals in the garden. Then Chang Ho had scarce been able to lift the smallest of the stone lions. Now, however, in his nineteenth year, he could with ease lift the largest one and hold it above his head at the full length of his arms— and that stone lion was heavier than the heaviest of Chang Fu Lung's soldiers.

There was a runway among the peach and mulberry trees where Chang Ho practised horseback riding, and many were the difficult feats he could perform. He could dismount easily and land on his feet with the horse at full gallop. He could stand erect in his saddle as the horse raced at top speed. He was a master horseman—better even than his father had been in his youth.

Chang Fu Lung watched Chang Ho, his eyes alight with pride and in the depths of them the burning fire of hope, as many friends came to speak with the old

148

general about his strong and dutiful son.

"He is old enough to marry," they told Chang Fu Lung, "and it is his duty to his Empire to take a bride and rear strong sons to serve His Majesty Chung Te."

"But he is still a mere boy," said Chang Fu Lung, "and there are yet many years before him in which he may wed and produce strong and valorous sons. He is to become a great general and he should not be troubled with the burdens a family would bring upon him."

This was almost heresy in a land where marriages were made early and all men reared huge families for their Emperor and to have sons to worship at their graves if they fell in battle; but Chang Fu Lung was so loyal to his Emperor and so high in His Majesty's confidence that his friends thought no evil of him.

But now that Chang Ho was nineteen, well beyond the age when young men should marry, there were many conferences in the *yamen* of Chang Fu Lung. Matchmakers came daily to speak with him—matchmakers sent by friends of the old general, friends who were fathers of comely and graceful daughters of the proper age. Chang Fu Lung temporized and really said no to none of them—which would have been extremely impolite. Neither, however, did he say yes.

But the meetings with matchmakers and royal couriers from the Throne now required many hours each day of the easily fatigued Chang Fu Lung so that in the garden Chang Ho performed his exercises alone. Of all those exercises, Chang Ho liked best the practise of archery—and as he shot his arrows at the target his thoughts were often far beyond the garden walls, abroad with the armies of His Majesty which Chang Ho one day hoped to command. He had no thought for other things. He was not interested in matchmakers or in maidens, because he never listened to the matchmakers who talked with his father and he knew no maidens save his own two sisters. Until, one day, fate took the reins of his destiny in hand as Chang Ho was practising at archery.

Arrow after arrow sped from his twanging bow and struck squarely in the center of the target, but his thoughts were so far away that it was not strange that, at last, one of his arrows merely touched the target enough to divert the arrow's flight and it sped like a streak of silver over the garden wall and into the garden of a neighbor.

Scarcely had his arrow dropped behind the wall, than from that direction came the sudden sound of weeping. Wildly Chang Ho, realizing that his arrow had caused injury to someone, looked about for a servant whom he might send to make inquiries; but his servants were gone for the moment from the garden, and there was nothing for Chang Ho to do but investigate in person.

It was the labor of but a second for him to leap upon one of the rockeries, close against the wall, and peer over. But the neighboring garden was so filled with trees that he could not even see the ground, though toward the center of the garden a goldfish pond gleamed radiant silver in the sun. From under the trees came still the sound of weeping. Chang Ho looked about him, remembering the proprieties. It was not well for a young man to enter, without permission, the garden of a neighbor. Yet that weeping was a maiden's weeping and the fault, he feared, was his own.

Chang Ho leaped to the top of the wall and dropped easily into the neighboring garden. Instantly, he saw a little maiden of perhaps fourteen years of age sitting disconsolately in a swing which swayed to and fro under the mulberry trees. Chang Ho sighed with relief. Surely none could criticize him for meeting a child of such tender years. Even in tears the little maiden was radiant. Her headdress was gorgeous—she might have been the daughter of a high official. Her cheeks were a delicate oval and her black eyebrows—

Chang Ho started. Her eyebrows! They were beautiful he knew, though just now it was difficult to make sure, for the right one was stained with crimson, and the fragile hand of the little maiden covered it as rubies of blood trickled through her fingers and fell upon her richly embroidered gown.

"May this humble person," began Chang Ho diffidently, "tell your exquisite person he is sorry that his ill-sped arrow struck you, and that no punishment is too great for him to suffer for causing you to weep so sadly?"

Frightened, the little maiden stood erect, swaying slightly on her tiny feet. Her hands went to her heart, and with deep compassion in his soul Chang Ho noted that the mark of one hand, etched in crimson, remained on her gown when, after a long moment in which she appeared undecided whether to flee or remain in the presence of this stranger, she lowered her hands and her dark eyes met those of Chang Ho.

"Your arrow, Exalted One," she said softly, "struck me here!"

She touched her right eyebrow and, instantly all contrition, Chang Ho stepped closer in order to see what damage his careless arrow had caused. It had broken the eyebrow so that, he knew, there would always be a scar and the beauty of this little maiden forever marred by one eyebrow divided in twain.

THE AMBER TALISMAN

She was a mere child and Chang Ho could see no harm in offering such comfort as he might. While he told her many stories, striving to make her smile through her tears, the maiden studied the person of Chang Ho and found him altogether pleasing. His black clothing fitted him closely. His arms were the mighty arms of a grown man, and his head like one done in bronze by a master craftsman. He was like a young god out of China's ancient legendry.

"Please tell me your honorable name," he begged her at last when she had dried her tears and the crimson rubies no longer fell from the wound above her eye.

"My despicable name, Exalted One," she told him, "is Silver Butterfly, and I will explain to my father your kindness when he asks what has happened to me. For, though your arrow hurt me until I wept with pain, the pain is gone because you are so kind, and my heart is filled with happiness because you are so gentle with me."

"Then," said Chang Ho boldly, "since the arrow brought me to you I am happy. Let us seek it together so that I may keep it forever as a symbol of sweet remembrance."

So they sought and found the arrow which had struck Silver Butterfly and had lodged deep in the trunk of a mulberry tree. Both trembled when they found it, for, had it struck more truly, it might have fatally injured Silver Butterfly.

Chang Ho held the arrow in his hand as they talked together. He told her of his dreams, of how he expected to become a great general; and Silver Butterfly, listening, watched his face all aglow with fervor and high ambition, and scarcely heard his words at all. He was so handsome and his eyes were like stars that laughed.

"Then, Exalted One," said Silver Butterfly at last, "you will soon depart from your father's garden, and —and—I shall never see you again."

"Yes, Silver Butterfly," he said, his lips smiling with eagerness, his eyes missing the cloud which crossed the lovely face of Silver Butterfly, "I shall soon depart to offer my services to His Majesty and the army."

Her little hands fluttered toward Chang Ho as though she would have touched his cheeks with the fingers of love's caress; but at that moment another maiden stepped from among the mulberry trees and paused in surprise. Silver Butterfly smiled shyly. There was a look of disapproval on the face of the newcomer.

"It is not proper, my precious little mistress," said the newcomer, "for your august self to talk with this

154

Exalted Stranger alone in the garden."

"This is Snowflake, my maid, Exalted One," explained Silver Butterfly, "and she is above all things loyal to me."

But the arrival of Snowflake had reminded both Chang Ho and Silver Butterfly of the proprieties and Chang Ho now began to make his preparations for departure.

As he turned to go Silver Butterfly, into whose heart the image of this stranger had crept as the minutes fled, sought for some excuse to stay him.

"Your necklace, Exalted One," she said, hurriedly, "is strangely wrought. May I see it?" Chang Ho, happy for some excuse to prolong the moment of departure, turned back and held forth the ornament.

"It is the necklace," he explained, "which my father placed about my neck when I was born—a piece of amber on a silver chain. My people believe that it is a symbol of good fortune and that nothing can ever befall me so long as I wear it."

Smiling shyly Silver Butterfly extended her hand to touch the necklace and Chang Ho, on a sudden impulse, slipped the silver chain from his neck and offered it to Silver Butterfly.

"As a token of my sorrow for hurting you," he said softly, "and to express my eternal hope for your endless good fortune and prosperity I give you this talisman. Keep it always to remind you that, wherever he may be, Chang Ho is sorry that he wounded you and that your image is enshrined forever in his heart!"

Silver Butterfly took the amulet and Chang Ho, turning to Snowflake, said:

"Guard your little mistress carefully, Snowflake. See that no harm comes to her and regard your own life as nothing if ever she is in danger."

Snowflake bowed deeply to the handsome young man and gave her promise to be loyal to Silver Butterfly. Chang Ho tore himself at last from the garden, mounting the wall and dropping within his own garden as lightly as a bird.

For many years Silver Butterfly did not see Chang Ho but always in her heart he held the hero's place. Always about her neck she wore the amber talisman and often she could fancy herself in the arms of Chang Ho as he had held her that day in the garden when he had stilled her weeping.

China was filled with trouble and, as bandits ravaged the country and laid waste the villages, Chang Ho became a man whose responsibilities seemed to have no end. It was rumored that he was in far Shantung. Then he was in Anhwei. Then he was in Pe-chihli—always at the head of His Majesty's army, to the command of which he had succeeded upon the death of Chang Fu Lung, gentle and full of years.

Always the vision of Silver Butterfly, when he had time to think of aught but fighting, was in the heart of Chang Ho.

"Two years have passed," Chang Ho, brow furrowed with care, would say to himself. "Silver Butterfly must be more beautiful than ever—and she is almost a woman."

"Chang Ho is a great hero," were the thoughts of Silver Butterfly, "and his victories are as many as his battles."

In the fourth year since Chang Ho had dropped over the garden wall, the mother and father of Silver Butterfly died and bandits descended upon the city in which they had lived so long and so peacefully. Silver Butterfly, with the faithful Snowflake at her side, fled in terror from the fury of the Red Beards —carrying with her all of gold and jewels that could be carried in her sleeves—and at last took up her residence in a far city.

With this treasure Silver Butterfly had bought a great house. Artisans had created for her a garden filled with gorgeous flowers, blossoming trees and all the delights to which she had ever been accustomed. Always in her heart was the hope that in some way she could help Chang Ho against the ever-increasing power of Wong Lao Hu, which meant the King of Tigers.

Many years passed and ill fortune followed His Majesty's army as the power of the bandit leader, Wong Lao Hu, became greater day by day. City after city, village after village, fell before his attacks. Men and women were given to the sword and cities looted. Silver Butterfly knew that the life of Chang Ho was filled with great trouble. There were even whispers, because failure so often attended his arms, that His Majesty Chung Te was meditating deeply about the loyalty of Chang Ho.

Silver Butterfly heard these rumors and her heart was afraid for Chang Ho, but there was nothing she could do save wait. Wait and dream of him.

She whiled away her time with her pet pigeons, of which she had many. At her bidding her servants fashioned little reeds of bamboo which they fastened to the legs or wings of the pigeons—hollow bits of bamboo, through which the wind made gentle music as the pigeons flew about the courtyard, and no matter how far they flew they were trained always to return, so that the garden became a place filled with the gentle music of bamboo reeds and the whirring of wings.

Though she did not know it, the fame of the beauty of Silver Butterfly had spread throughout the Empire, and the stories said that the tiny scar above her right eye but added to her beauty—and all these stories came at last to the evil ears of Wong Lao Hu, the leader of the bandits, by now a mighty army at the killer's back.

One morning, without warning, Wong Lao Hu descended upon the village of Chiaochung. The villagers fled in terror, only to discover that the forces of Wong Lao Hu had surrounded the village and that there was no escape. Sullen black smoke from burning houses darkened the sky. Over all rose the cries of the dying and the voices of women begging for mercy.

But Silver Butterfly was not afraid, though even her pigeons were frightened and she caused her servants to place them in their great cage before she gave them permission to flee and try to save themselves. Snowflake, her face pale, but her heart high with courage, remained beside her mistress. In her bosom she carried a dagger.

"That we may slay ourselves if the evil hands of Wong Lao Hu should touch us, my mistress," she explained quietly.

Silver Butterfly scarcely heard her. The word of

the slaughter in Chiaochung would spread throughout the Empire—and the army of Chang Ho would surely come to the rescue of the city, or at least in pursuit of the bandits as they fled to the hills to divide their loot.

Within an hour after Wong Lao Hu had attacked the city it was in his possession. He chose the residence of Silver Butterfly as his own, because it was the best in the village. He entered it at the head of a hundred of his most sturdy archers—and stopped in amazement when his greedy eyes fell upon Silver Butterfly, head held proudly erect, unafraid, with Snowflake beside her.

"Ho! Ho!" he laughed. "Ha! Ha! So the beautiful Silver Butterfly has come to the net of Wong Lao Hu at last! Make ready, little butterfly of silver, to depart into the hills with your master!"

Silver Butterfly turned to Snowflake.

"Tell this low person," she said, "that if he so much as compels me to hold words with him it is my duty to commit suicide! I am unmarried and even to exchange words with a man means degradation which only death can atone for."

Again Wong Lao Hu laughed, uproariously.

"Tell your butterfly mistress, ugly maid," said Wong Lao Hu, his voice harsh and filled with evil, "that Wong Lao Hu does not believe in this pretentious culture, and that in the far hills where he lives he will cause Silver Butterfly to forget it, too."

So all words that passed between Wong Lao Hu and Silver Butterfly were delivered through Snowflake, and Wong Lao Hu was tolerant. But he seemed eager, because of Silver Butterfly, to flee to the hills. He told her his plans, and through Snowflake she curtly refused to go with him; but he gave commands to his men, who laid violent hands upon her and carried her away. She did not know that her amber talisman had been broken in the struggle, until hours later when thoughts of Chang Ho caused her hand to stray to where the necklace always hung.

Wong Lao Hu had laughed at her one sobbing request—that her pigeons be taken with her into the hills.

"Why," he asked her boldly, "should you take pigeons with you for amusement when all the days of Wong Lao Hu, henceforth, shall be devoted to your pleasure?"

But his many servants had lightly borne along the cage containing the pigeons. After all Wong Lao Hu was a great soldier—and a great murderer—and he could well afford to please Silver Butterfly in a matter so trivial.

Three days afterward, when the army of Wong Lao Hu was vanishing into its hiding place in the hills—the army of Chang Ho, exhausted from the mighty march they had made to reach stricken Chiaochung entered the ruined village. The heart of Chang Ho was heavy, for failure had followed upon failure so often that he could expect at any moment a courier from His Majesty Chung Te, relieving him of command of the army, setting another in his place and perhaps even ordering Chang Ho to the capital of the Middle Kingdom for punishment as a traitor.

"If only," he told himself, "some good fortune were to deliver Wong Lao Hu into my hands."

He made his headquarters in the best house remaining in Chiaochung—the house of Silver Butterfly. The furniture in it had been broken, the walls torn and defaced and the hands of the vandals had left their marks everywhere. The ruined interior of the house was typical of the ruins of Chiaochung, which it now became the task of Chang Ho to repair and make whole again. He must bury the dead and make safe the village so that the few inhabitants who had escaped might again return to their homes.

Gloomily he walked through the house and as he passed slowly through the reception room something slipped under his foot. Curious about the smallest thing in this desolate place he stooped and lifted from the floor a silver chain and a broken piece of amber!

There was a character on the bit of amber though only part of it remained, but Chang Ho did not need to see the entire character to know it. How had the talisman come here? What evil gods had brought Silver Butterfly into the wicked hands of Wong Lao Hu? Where was she now?

Late that evening, when darkness had fallen on the ruined village, one of Silver Butterfly's servants came creeping back and told the story. Wong Lao Hu had carried her off into the hills. But there were many hills. An army thrice the size of Chang Ho's might search the hills for many moons and still not find the hiding place of Wong Lao Hu.

"But she has been gone for three days, at the very least," moaned Chang Ho, "and she must long since have slain herself if Wong Lao Hu has so much as touched her with his hands. Wong Lao Hu would but laugh at her threats to slay herself! No, the Silver Butterfly is dead! But I shall follow and avenge her —and destroy Wong Lao Hu! Tonight my army shall rest, and tomorrow we shall march into the hills!"

Chang Ho gathered his officers about him and told them what he intended.

"But we must travel in small bands," they objected,

"in order to search everywhere. How shall the rest of the army know when a searching party, traveling always at night, has located the hiding place of the King of Tigers? If we build a signal fire Wong Lao Hu will also see it and will come and slay those who build it."

"I shall think of a plan," said Chang Ho. "Let our soldiers sleep and I shall spend the night in thought."

And while the shadows grew long across the courtyard which must have hearkened often to the sweet voice and gentle laughter of Silver Butterfly, Chang Ho paced the floor of the house that had covered her.

His heart was in torment as he thought of what might be happening in the distant hills—of the terrible things that might even now mean disaster to Silver Butterfly.

And then a strange musical sound fell upon his ears. It sounded like the far playing of a tiny flute. It came from the sky above the courtyard, a whispering sound and the fluttering of tiny wings. The sound ceased. A servant of Silver Butterfly entered, bowing, his face filled with sorrow, holding in his arms a pigeon. The bird was almost dead. Its eyes seemed to weep; its wings were bedraggled, its legs torn and bleeding.

"It is one of the pets of little mistress, Silver Butter-

164

fly," explained the servant. "She took her pigeons with her into the hills. See? There is the bamboo reed which made the piping sound. I know it because I fashioned it for little mistress with my own hands."

Chang Ho ordered water and food for the pigeon and took the tired bird in his hands.

"If only, belled pigeon," he said as he gently stroked the feathers of the bird, "you could speak and tell me where to find your mistress!"

The pigeon whose white lids covered its tired eyes raised them and seemed to look into the eyes of Chang Ho and, suddenly, he knew that it did bear a message!

His heart beating high with excitement, Chang Ho carefully examined the pigeon, parting its bedraggled feathers to search. And so he found the message at last—characters roughly made on a piece of rice paper, folded small and fastened under the pigeon's wing. His hands trembled as Chang Ho read the characters.

"The valley of my prison," said the characters, "is very deep and at either end is a great hummock of stone, one shaped as a monster stone lion, like those you once lifted in your garden. May your strength be great enough to lift this one! The other hummock is like a camel, with its head in the clouds. But alas! I know not the location of this valley!"

Now Chang Ho leaped up and shouted to his officers.

"Bring me the men of the village!" he commanded. "Bring me men who know the hills!"

Hours passed as he asked questions of the villagers and with each passing hour the piping, flutelike sounds broke again and again over the courtyard, and more pigeons, all exhausted as though they had flown fast and far, fluttered into the garden which belonged to Silver Butterfly.

"Make haste!" said one message. "Oh, make haste! For I am worn and suffering! I stand on a precipice, bidding Wong Lao Hu not to touch me else I shall leap over to the rocks below! This is my last message! I have lost the talisman and good fortune has deserted me!"

When he read this last message the heart of Chang Ho was filled with great and awful fury.

Dawn was silvering the east and still he asked his endless questions. But at last there came a man who was very old—a man who knew the hills because he had roamed through them as a hunter. He recalled a valley where a lion of stone crouched at one end while at the other a camel of stone reared its head into the clouds.

There was a precipice, at whose base, far, far below, there were great boulders. One who fell among them would be broken into the smallest pieces.

He promised to guide the army of Chang Ho to the valley, and Chang Ho gave orders that the army be ready to march when the sun went down—bearing only their bows and arrows and wearing nothing that would make a sound in the stillness of the night. Then, while the sun crawled down the heavens into the west, he shut himself in a room and would see no one. When night fell at last he came forth to lead his army, dressed as simply as the least of his soldiers, and was himself armed with bow and arrows.

The army began the march to the hills—and it marched faster than it had ever marched before. It must not, Chang Ho ordered, even stop for a breathing space. It must reach the valley of mystery before sunrise, so that it would pass through a sleeping country and folk would not rise and race ahead of Chang Ho to take warning to Wong Lao Hu.

The cold of the dawn was an icy cold. Silver Butterfly, with the faithful Snowflake at her side, sat at the very lip of the precipice. Now and again they peered over, fearfully, into the awful depths. Then they would look back at the minions of Wong Lao Hu who squatted, ever watchful, in a semicircle about

167

them to see that they did not escape. Wong Lao Hu had threatened them with death if Silver Butterfly escaped. If she plunged to the rocks below, they would be compelled to follow her. If she escaped otherwise, they would be hurled over to destruction. So they did not sleep—for Wong Lao Hu was a bandit who kept his word.

It was dark and cold and the heart of Silver Butterfly was heavy with despair.

"When morning comes, little Snowflake," she said, "Wong Lao Hu will come for me at last. He does not believe that I will leap to death and will try to put hands upon me."

"Have courage," whispered Snowflake, "for I shall go with you and hold your hand in mine. Death will be quick and merciful—and far more honorable than that the hands of Wong Lao Hu should touch you."

"I should even leap now," said Silver Butterfly, "because the hands of men have touched me."

"But through no fault of yours, my poor little mistress," replied Snowflake. "Surely none would blame you for something you could not prevent. What is the strength of Silver Butterfly against the strength of the minions of the King of Tigers?"

So they waited. Their bodies were stiff and cold. With the first mantle of gold in the east, heralding the

168

rising sun, Wong Lao Hu came from his hut in the hills, with an evil smile on his face, like a wolf that seeks its prey.

Quickly his men rose and stretched themselves as the leader approached. He snarled curt commands at them and they departed swiftly, grinning back at Silver Butterfly and Snowflake.

"Silver Butterfly," said Wong Lao Hu, halting abruptly as Silver Butterfly and Snowflake rose, "I have come for you. Let Snowflake choose a mate from among my soldiers; but only their leader, the Tiger King, is fit mate for the Silver Butterfly whose beauty is a legend in the Middle Kingdom. Think, Silver Butterfly! My wealth is as the wealth of the Empire! At my tiger cry the Emperor himself cringes and is afraid! I can prepare palaces for you and you shall be great in all the land."

Slowly Wong Lao Hu, as he spoke, moved forward. Fearfully Silver Butterfly and Snowflake peered over into the abyss and, while their eyes were turned from him, Wong Lao Hu sprang toward them, his great hands clutching for the gown of Silver Butterfly.

But even as his hands would have touched her gown, a great scream burst from the throat of Wong Lao Hu. Snowflake, more watchful than her mistress, had seen the figure in the dusk behind him. She cried out to Silver Butterfly, caught at her gown and pulled her toward her as Wong Lao Hu, clutching at empty space, tottered on the edge of the precipice.

Then, screaming again, a strangled scream that died away as he fell, Wong Lao Hu plunged down to the far, harsh rocks below.

Holding each other closely, Silver Butterfly and Snowflake watched the fall of the man who would have destroyed them both.

"Look!" whispered Snowflake. "See the arrow in his back! It struck him just as his hands would have touched you, little mistress!"

They turned away as Wong Lao Hu struck the rocks below, and out of the growing dawn strode the godlike figure of Chang Ho, his bow clasped in his hands. He placed his bow and arrows on the rocks and held forth his empty arms for Silver Butterfly.

She did not see that the walls about the valley were darkened by the forms of men. She did not hear the screams of the bandits of Wong Lao Hu as thousands of arrows came out of the darkness to strike them down. She saw only the face and form of her beloved, which she had carried in her heart down the years. Chang Ho held in his arms again the little maiden whose broken right eyebrow had caused them so much sorrow. Lost in the joy of reunion they stood while his men put to rout the followers of Wong Lao Hu.

"My belled pigeons?" she whispered at last, her words muffled against the heart of Chang Ho. "They returned home?"

Chang Ho could only nod. His eyes were fixed broodingly upon the black rim of that awful precipice which had almost taken Silver Butterfly.

"Silver Butterfly," he said softly, "you have helped me to make whole and safe again His Majesty's Empire—and my reward will be great. But it would be as nothing without you."

"I thought," whispered Silver Butterfly, "that my good fortune had fled from me forever—for when I was captured by Wong Lao Hu my amber talisman was broken and lost!"

"And it is lost forever," said Chang Ho softly, "though I am glad beyond all gladness that it is. I used the bit of amber to fashion a tip for the arrow which slew the King of Tigers. We no longer need the talisman—for it could never benefit us more than it has! It has brought us the greatest good fortune we could ever possess; it has brought us together and destroyed our enemy!"

When Chang Ho's soldiers brought the sedan chair

which had borne Silver Butterfly into the mountains it was a signal that the valley of terror had been purged entirely of evil, and Silver Butterfly, with a whole army as escort and Chang Ho striding like a king beside her chair, rode smiling and happy down the mountainside while the sun came up and smiled upon them all—even upon the loyal Snowflake who rode easily upon the shoulders of two of her new master's sturdiest soldiers.

DELICATE PEONY OF WU

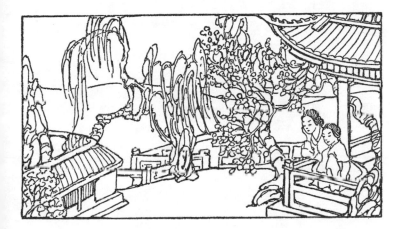

DELICATE PEONY OF WU

REES bordered the valley highway curving its course through the heart of the Kingdom of Wu and made a leafy screen to protect from curious eyes the magnificent gardens of the home where dwelt the maiden, Delicate Peony, whose parents had long since ascended the Dragon Throne on High. Old servants who had attended upon her father and mother now served the maiden faithfully, and her secluded days were happy.

Delicate Peony was content to while away the hours of sunshine in her garden, studying the Classics of ancient times or playing with her little sleeve-dog, Snow, a mischievous creature who loved to chase any moving object. Sometimes when she walked near the trees that shut her garden off from the highway, she could hear the passing of chair-bearers, the rumbling of carts and the singsong chanting of coolies—her only contact with the outside world.

Then she would recall the days when her father had been a high official at the court of Wu and when she had often listened to long discussions of matters

relating to the court. From these remembered con-
versations she was able to imagine pictures of the
world outside, of the people who lived in it, and of
the pomp and ceremony of life at court.

Sometimes she dreamed of how marvelous it would
be to be a queen. She knew that she was beautiful.
Her mirror told her that when she made her morning toilet, and the quiet pools in her gardens, beside
which she often sat, gave back reflections of her
lovely face. Her gowns were exquisite creations of
gold, of silver, of purple or of soft scarlet like her
lips, and when she studied herself in the waters of
the pools, from her tiny shoes, which showed beneath
the hem of her gown, to the jeweled headdress which
hid her hair of raven blackness, she wondered. Perhaps, some day, if she wished enough and kept herself
beautiful and filled her heart with knowledge, her
dream might come true.

Meanwhile she was content to wait. In her gardens
was sunshine; the droning of bees made gentle music
and the fragrance of countless flowers filled the days.
A place of happiness and peace.

On the face of Delicate Peony when she slept
there was always a faint smile which none ever saw
save the old woman servant who came in late to make
sure that her heart's treasure slept well.

"May you always be happy, little flower," the old woman invariably whispered, as her gnarled hands smoothed the coverlets.

Then she would glide softly out of the chamber of Delicate Peony and join her aged husband.

"Does the little flower smile tonight?" he always asked.

"She smiled in her sleep," his wife would answer, "and all is right with her. Her life is joyous and her sleep is gentle because her heart is in the middle."

"Yes," her husband would agree. "Her heart is in the middle, which, as everyone knows, is the right place for a maiden's heart to be."

But not so many *li* distant, outside of the valley, beyond the hills that rose against the sky, happiness had departed and slumbers were fitful. This was at the court of Chun Te, King of Wu, whose wives were many and beautiful and whose courtiers were so richly garbed that they shone like the sun. Chun Te was a ruler who loved his people, and he had ruled them for their happiness, giving no thought to war. Now fear haunted Chun Te and his ministers, because of the rapacity of Han Huang Te, ruler of the neighboring Kingdom of Yueh, and his reported greed for more kingdoms to rule.

Chun Te called his ministers about him and they came, lines of anxiety carven on their faces, and fell to their knees before their ruler. All knew why they had been bidden this morning to audience with His Majesty. Many stories had come to their ears of Han Huang Te and his mighty kingdom, and all of these stories were fearful.

Chun Te raised his jewel-covered hand and bade his ministers stand to hear his words.

"We have hearkened to the tales from the Kingdom of Yueh," His Majesty said. "And the schemes of Han Huang Te are not hidden from us. He is greedy for Wu because it borders Yueh, and because the two kingdoms, united under his dominion, would be invincible against the remaining three kingdoms. Our heart is filled with trouble and we know not what to do. Han Huang Te comes often to hold speech with us, and always his words are those of a friend—even while his retainers spy upon our kingdom and decide how best they may attack and take it. We have brought you here to listen to your words in the matter and to condescend to hearken to your advice. What have you to tell us?"

The ministers stared fearfully at one another and shifted uneasily on their feet, for this was an audience

filled with portent. Then the Grand Councilor, oldest and wisest of all the officials at the court of Chun
Te, spoke.

"For many moons, Your Majesty," he said in his
cracked ancient voice, "the minds of your loyal ministers have been upon this matter, and we are agreed
that we know not what to do. In the moon which is
soon upon us, His Majesty, Han Huang Te comes
again to pretend friendship with Your Majesty, and
rumors say that he brings almost an army at his
back. Before he comes we must consider every plan
and reject none, however simple. This humble person, Your Majesty's Grand Councilor, has not been
idle. He has found an aged one who may perhaps ad-
vise us what to do. Tsao Fu is his lowly name, and
he is a seer whose fame is known through all the five
kingdoms. He reads the future in the stars and in
the waters of the earth. This slave of Your Majesty's
begs leave to bid the soothsayer into your august
presence."

Chun Te agreed with a slight nod of his head.
His brows were furrowed with thought because the
case was altogether desperate. Eunuchs repeated the
name of Tsao Fu until it reached him in the outer
courtyard. Then into His Majesty's presence came
an aged man whose eyes were bright with wisdom,

whose beard was long upon his breast, whose shoulders were bowed beneath a weight that none could see.

"This despicable old one, Your Majesty," he murmured as he knelt to perform the customary genuflections to his sovereign, "is named Tsao Fu, and it is his wish to serve the Kingdom of Wu and its mightiest of rulers."

"Rise, Tsao Fu. It is in our hearts to hear your words. Speak then, and tell us of the fate of Wu."

Tsao Fu bade the eunuchs bring him a certain bowl of which he knew. This was a bowl of white jade—ancient jade stained with streaks like yellow gold. The bowl was older even than the Kingdom of Wu and Yueh. Hundreds of years ago it had been taken from the grave of an all-wise sage of the past and given into the keeping of the ancestors of Chun Te. The bowl was filled to the brim with water and placed upon a tabouret before the kneeling Tsao Fu.

"The truth, Tsao Fu!" said His Majesty. "The truth and nothing else, whether it be good or evil in our ears."

"The truth shall be told, Your Majesty," replied Tsao Fu. "May this humble person ask that all keep silent while he reads the future from the white jade bowl?"

Silence fell in the court of Chun Te. Not even a whisper passed among the eunuchs, who in other times were never silent, and the ministers stood like graven images.

"Hearken," began the aged Tsao Fu in a voice that they must strain their ears to hear, "while this humble person speaks of the future. The Kingdom of Wu shall be saved, but saved only at grave danger to a woman's life and honor. Within the jade bowl there is a maiden's face, beautiful beyond words of this despicable one to express. These eyes have never seen the maiden, but she sits alone, playing with a little sleeve-dog, in a garden near the highway that curves between the Kingdoms of Wu and Yueh. She is like a queen upon a throne. There will be no war with Yueh and no shedding of blood if this maiden of rare loveliness be found."

"Is the maiden known to us?" asked Chun Te.

"Your Majesty has never beheld her."

"Are there any among my ministers who know this maiden?" continued the ruler.

"There are many of us who know her," came the reluctant voice of the Grand Councilor. "She is Delicate Peony, daughter of the illustrious general who fought to create the Kingdom of Wu for

Your Majesty's father. If the maiden's father yet lived we might dare to cast defiance at the King of Yueh. To this great man the Kingdom of Wu owes a debt that is ill repaid by asking his daughter to endanger life and honor."

The face of Chun Te hardened.

"It is for the kingdom," he said sternly. "Go forth and speak with this Delicate Peony, and bring us news of her before Han Huang Te comes to pay his visit of deceit."

So the Grand Councilor and many other ministers who were old and had known well the father of Delicate Peony journeyed that day down the curving highway that led from Wu to Yueh, along which way was the home of Delicate Peony. They entered the courtyard with bowed heads and hearts heavy with sorrow. And because the Grand Councilor was old and Delicate Peony had known him since she could remember aught at all, the ministers begged him to act as spokesman.

In the mighty dwelling which had been her father's and now was hers, Delicate Peony listened to the words of the Grand Councilor.

"The meaning, little flower," he said sadly, "of what Tsao Fu saw in the white jade bowl is all too plain. Who does not know that Han Huang Te—

may his line be accursed forever!—is greedy for wide domains and greedier still for women who are beautiful. He will desire your loveliness and you must go with him into Yueh. There you must try to divert him from his purpose of despoiling Wu, and you must send word of his plans to us by our spies."

"It is for the country of my august father—the country which I love," said Delicate Peony softly. "And a life is little, after all, to give for Wu."

"But Han Huang Te will take you as a Secondary Wife, little flower!" warned the Grand Councilor. "It will be worse for you than death, since he is a man you will always hate because he desires the ruin of the country you love as your noble father loved it."

"Unto sorrow and degradation—even unto worse than death—will this humble Delicate Peony go for Wu's sake," she replied. "Tell me, old friend of my father, am I beautiful enough to find favor in the eyes of the King of Yueh?"

"More beautiful than the sunset," exclaimed the Grand Councilor, "more gorgeous than the rainbows that arch the sky when storms are at an end!"

"Then bid Your Majesty await without fear the

approaching visit of Han Huang Te, for this humble person has a plan which may succeed, and if it does the kingdom may yet be free from the greedy ruler of Yueh."

Finally the day came which was set for the visit of Han Huang Te to Wu. Filled with determination, Delicate Peony rose that fateful morning and garbed herself in robes so rich that she might in truth have been the queen of her day-dreams. From tiny shoes to jeweled headdress she was a vision of loveliness. Her eyes were starry with excitement beneath brows like the wings of tiny sable moths, and in the pallor of her beautiful face her lips were vivid as ripe cherries.

When all was done to her satisfaction she sent a servant for Snow, her little sleeve-dog. Holding the wriggling little creature in her arms, she slowly made her way to that part of the gardens nearest the highway along which Han Huang Te and his retinue must pass.

At last they came. Sedan chairs of gold and purple. Outriders garbed in glory that rivalled the sun. A royal cavalcade. Delicate Peony, her heart dead within her, but her purpose unshaken, knew what she must do. Her breast was rising and fall-

ing like the surging of a wind, but her eyes were
filled with a look which boded ill for Han Huang Te.
She watched for the coming of his golden regal chair
and then—

Snow, the little dog, suddenly released from irk-
some bondage, darted swift as an arrow toward the
moving cavalcade, his bark shrilling through the
morning. And after him, scarcely any less swift, came
his mistress, breaking through the protecting screen
of trees and swaying on tiny shoes to rescue her
pet.

Outriders pulled up their horses and chair-bearers
halted their steps at this most amazing appearance of
a beautiful maiden, richly dressed and obviously of
noble birth, a maiden whose face would ordinarily be
shielded from any public gaze.

Just as Delicate Peony snatched up her little
sleeve-dog, the gold curtains of the regal chair were
thrust aside and a face looked out, a young face,
handsome and arrogant, darkened now with anger
over this unexplained delay. For a moment Delicate
Peony was motionless, as if overcome with horror at
the realization of what she had done, and in that moment the eyes of Han Huang Te peered deeply into
hers. His expression changed from anger to amazement and in his eyes little lights began to grow and

glow. Suddenly the spell was broken. Delicate Peony turned and ran back through the trees, while the cavalcade, at Han Huang's bidding, moved on to the court of Chun Te.

Later that day the two kings spoke together, and their words were friendly, but Chan Te felt that behind the apparent friendliness of Han Huang Te a multitude of swords was hidden.

"I am minded," the visiting ruler said, "to be forever the friend of Chun Te and his Kingdom of Wu. But to make the bond between us lasting there should be a living symbol at the court of Yueh of the good will of Wu."

"Above many riches my kingdom will prize the friendship of Yueh," Chun Te replied. "What then is this living symbol of which you speak?"

"In my palace, as in yours, Chun Te, there are many beautiful flowers of womanhood, and it is my custom to add to their number any maiden of rare loveliness encountered on my travels. Such a maiden there is in your kingdom, one whose gardens border the highway where lately my train passed by. With one of my bearers for guide, bid your slaves seek out and bring before you this treasure among maidens. Then deliver her into my hands that she may be the living sign—

the covenant of peace between us."

"Your wish shall be our pleasure," said Chun Te, and he sent slaves to bring Delicate Peony to his court.

So it came about that Delicate Peony stood before Chun Te and his royal guest, into whose eyes she had so lately gazed. But now her eyes were downcast as she listened to the words of her august ruler.

"As a living symbol of peace between the two kingdoms we give you, Delicate Peony. From this moment you belong to His Majesty, Han Huang Te of Yueh. And you depart forever from our kingdom to reside during our brother king's pleasure within the borders of Yueh."

Delicate Peony's eyes were still cast down, hidden under lowered lashes so long that they rested on her flushed cheeks.

"Never to return to Wu!" she murmured. "Never to return to the country which is my love, my treasure!"

The eyes of Han Huang Te lighted with pleasure. Delicate Peony had spoken only of sorrow in leaving her kingdom. There had been no word of reluctance about going with him. Perhaps he had found favor in the eyes of this maiden whom he now saw to be even

187

lovelier than his memory of her.

"The gods have been good in granting us such a gift as you, Delicate Peony," he said. "Sorrow not for your country of Wu, for with us you shall be happy and forget. But if sad longings should come, remember that all things are possible to Han Huang Te. Wherever you wish we will build a watchtower so high that from its crest you can look beyond the horizon into the heart of Wu."

Then Delicate Peony raised her eyes to her lord's and smiled.

And so, with a smile on her lips but in her mind the thought that she would find a way to thwart the plans of Han Huang Te, Delicate Peony returned in his cavalcade to Yueh. After her departure from Wu, Chun Te's Grand Councilor chose loyal spies who should attend upon her in secret and return at her bidding with news of what transpired in Yueh.

Still smiling, she was wedded to Han Huang Te, with hate in her heart for him because of his plots against her country. And ever her spies went to and fro between Yueh and Wu. From her messages Chun Te discovered a way by which Yueh might be destroyed, even while its ruler plotted against Wu. He set plans in motion and looked to the matter of secretly creating an army.

Many moons passed and Han Huang Te found that he loved Delicate Peony deeply and reverently. There was nothing she could ask of him that she might not have. But although the stolen flower of Wu appeared to love him dutifully, in the heart of Han Huang Te was a vague discontent, a feeling that the real Delicate Peony always eluded him.

Moved by the greatness of his devotion to her, Han Huang Te made Delicate Peony his First Wife, upon whom all the others at court must wait as servants. In the heart of this one-time warrior was now nothing but love for Delicate Peony. In her he possessed the world. He thought no longer of conquest, had forgotten his desire for possession of Wu. But always there was the sense of something which eluded his love, and this troubled Han Huang Te more than the cares and worries of his kingdom. Was she pining for her country of Wu? She had never held him to his promise, and the watchtower from which she could look into Wu had never been built.

There was something that troubled Delicate Peony. But what could it be? Often he walked in the gardens, pondering upon this thing which was hidden from him. When he asked her she always shook her head and would not speak. But there came a time when Han Huang Te was to solve the mystery, and, solving it, to bring upon his heart a pang worse than death.

One evening he was striding softly through the gardens when the sound of weeping came to him. He paused in the shadows and listened. It was a woman who wept, and the heart of Han Huang Te was stricken as he recognized the voice of Delicate Peony. Hurrying toward the sound of weeping, he came upon her.

"What is it, my heart's treasure?" he cried in deep distress. Delicate Peony lifted her eyes to his. Tears glistened on her cheeks and shone in the eyes she raised to him. For a long moment she remained speechless on her knees before Han Huang Te. Then words came.

"Slay me, my lord," she cried. "Slay me because I am a traitor, doubly a traitor, since I am false both to Wu and to Yueh. Know that this thrice-to-be-despised Delicate Peony came hither to Yueh with hatred in her heart for you. Know that she came to plot your ruin if she could. Know that for many moons she has sent her spies to Wu—"

The heart of Han Huang Te became suddenly cold. The flame of love which consumed him turned to ashes and the light in his eyes died.

"It was a plot from the very beginning," Delicate Peony continued wildly, "a plot that you should see and desire me, that you should take me from Wu, so that my country should have a spy in your very palace. It was a plot to destroy Yueh by trickery, to make your kingdom weak, to make it forget its army, so that Wu should have time to grow in strength and then turn upon Yueh. See, I tell you all. Slay me, I beseech you."

"Then why," queried Han Huang Te, "has not the army of Wu attacked Yueh?"

"Because I bade them wait until the time was ripe for Yueh to be utterly despoiled. I bade them wait my word that the time for Yueh's destruction was at hand."

"And why have you not sent this word, little flower?"

"Because I have learned that there is something more precious to me than the welfare of Wu, more precious than all the world. After my betrayal of your kingdom I have learned that I who hated you have grown to love you beyond life, beyond death. I know that I shall be happy in death, if death shall come by your loved hands. Take then this dagger and thrust it into the heart that now holds but the thought of you —my master—my beloved!"

Crushed with the realization of what she had done,

Delicate Peony did not see how the lights came back into the eyes of Han Huang Te. She only saw the dagger she had thrust into his right hand, and bared her breast over her heart. A faint smile trembled on her lips, a smile because she was to die by the hand of her lord whom she loved.

Han Huang Te looked at the shining dagger in his hand, then flung it far from him. Kneeling beside Delicate Peony, his arms went about her and drew her close.

"I understand the weight of your sorrow, my little flower," he murmured. "For in all the world the most difficult decision is between two loves—especially when honor is weighed in the balance. But know this, my heart. One thing above all others I have wished to hear; one thing I have prayed the gods of heaven to set upon your lips, and only now am I answered. For at last I have heard this thing, and after these words that you have spoken all other words are empty of meaning. You have said that you love me. What matter kingdoms then?"

For a time their happiness was so great that they knew only that they were lovers, that the garden was filled with a thousand evening perfumes, and that the gentle moon was smiling down upon them. But at last Delicate Peony remembered.

"Chun Te!" she cried. "He awaits but my word to march with his army against your kingdom."

"Is your love for Wu still as great as it was?"

"There is but one thing greater, greater beyond all counting, my love for my master and my king!"

"Then perhaps there is a way. Send the promised word to Chun Te. Tell him that he is to march on Yueh when four moons shall have passed, in the middle of the fifth moon hence. But as your love is true, do not tell him that I shall meet him at the border with my army. Bid him come by the road that curves between our two kingdoms."

"There will be war!" cried Delicate Peony. "Blood will be shed and all the fault is mine!"

Han Huang Te shook his head and smiled a little.

"I shall hold speech with Chun Te," he said, "and it is in my heart that when the story is told there will be no war and no bloodshed. But it is also in my heart to wish that the armies of Wu and of Yueh shall witness the thing which I plan and shall hear the words which pass between Han Huang Te and Chun Te. I shall lead my army, and you, most fragrant of flowers, shall journey with me."

Then, for four moons, though he smiled when she asked him questions, Han Huang Te would not tell her what he planned.

But the day finally came when two armies faced each other at the border between Yueh and Wu. And Delicate Peony, peering from her curtained sedan chair, marveled at a building which stood by the way and which had not been there when she had passed by on her journey to Yueh. Beneath its golden roof it was gorgeous beyond even her dreams of beauty.

Chun Te came forth as his army halted, and Han Huang Te went out to meet him, so that their encounter was between the two armies. And when the two kings met, Han Huang Te raised his voice to speak so that he was easily heard by all.

"Behold this house of the golden roof, O Chun Te, my brother. Behold it well all ye who hear our words. Know, all of you, that it rests upon the border between Yueh and Wu—that half of it is in Yueh and the other half in Wu. It is our wish for peace between the kingdoms, so we have caused this palace to be erected here in secret, as a symbol of the peace for which we long. With us rides a maiden of Wu who loved her country with all her heart, loved it so much that she would have betrayed Yueh, had she not learned that she loved Han Huang Te, whom she had regarded as an enemy. She is the rarest treasure of Wu which you have given into our hands to be our queen, Chun Te, my brother. Let there be peace between us because we are one family, one people. And let this palace of the golden roof be the symbol of the unity of Wu and Yueh in bonds that may never be severed.

"Delicate Peony would have given her life for Wu's sake. We have returned that life to her for Yueh. Yueh is our kingdom, and if Delicate Peony were to die the world would be empty for us and the suffering of Yueh's people would fall on ears deaf to hear them. Therefore let all know that Delicate Peony would have died for Wu's sake, and that she lives for the sake of Yueh! And the palace in which she may live in Yueh, yet journey into Wu when she desires, is here before the eyes of all of you who hear us, symbol of a love that is greater than the hates of men, greater than the glory of war, greater than the ambition of kings! Shall we then have peace, Chun Te, whom we would call brother?"

Chun Te did not reply in words. He placed his right hand on the left shoulder of Han Huang Te. Then Han Huang Te placed his right hand on the left shoulder of Chun Te. The two kings turned and moved side by side toward the palace of the golden roof— while behind them their armies cast aside their arms and smiled upon each other.

Before the door of the palace Chun Te and Han Tuang Te paused and bowed deeply in reverent genuflection. Thus they did honor to the happiest woman in Yueh or in Wu, as smiling chair-bearers carried the chair of Delicate Peony past them, into the palace of the roof of gold.

THE HONORABLE FIVE
BLESSINGS

THE HONORABLE FIVE
BLESSINGS

GOLDEN BAMBOO sat motionless in the bow of her father's fishing boat, her slender hands curled together on her knees, her red lips slightly parted, her eyes dreaming of something far away. So deep was this waking dream it made her forget for the moment that she could no longer wear a headdress, but must coil her hair like a black serpent on her shapely head; that her gown, once so bright and beautiful, now was faded and old.

In the center of Lake Hangchow the huge pagoda on the island rose from the deep blue waters like some gorgeous solitary flower, and over the lake, muted by distance to music, came the voices of the people of Hangchow, enjoying a perpetual holiday. From the shores of the lake the tree-clothed mountains reached away to the edges of the world, and villages kowtowed at their feet. Temple bells sounded from near and far, their chiming softened across the waters.

Golden Bamboo sighed a little, returning from her dream. She looked over the side of the fishing boat to where its shadow rode along below the surface. A jeweled fish swam into the shadow and out again.

"August father," said Golden Bamboo softly, "this very instant I saw a beautiful *samli* swim past beneath our boat. He was a great proud creature and a prize for you to capture."

Her father, Mung Ting, an old man in the garments of a Hangchow fisherman did not answer, and she looked toward him in surprise. Just now he was not fishing at all, but merely looking at his daughter, who was radiant despite the shabbiness of her faded gown.

"Did you not hear me, august father?" asked Golden Bamboo.

"I heard you, my daughter. However, I do not think of *samli*, but of all the things I saw just now looking out of your eyes, when you were gone to some far place in your dreams. All my life I shall reproach myself for having failed a daughter so utterly beautiful, a daughter who should have wed in all honor the greatest noble in the Middle Kingdom."

Mung Ting made an end of speaking and his gnarled hands fumbled a little with his nets. Golden

Bamboo could see in his face that he did not think of fish, though the taking of the best fish of Hangchow, to grace the tables of the wealthy, provided food and a dwelling place for Mung Ting and his daughter.

"You must not trouble about me, august father," said Golden Bamboo, her smile showing teeth that were white as snow, "for I am happier here on Hangchow Lake with you than I could ever be in the palace of China's greatest noble or even of His Majesty the Emperor!"

"You must not speak so lightly of His Majesty!" said Mung Ting. "To speak lightly of the Emperor might cause us both to suffer untold sorrow and hardship, perhaps even death."

"There is none abroad on the lake to hear, O my father," said Golden Bamboo, smiling again. "And why should you be so loyal, august father, to this Emperor who listened to the lying words of his dishonest Premier and banished you from the court you had served so long and well?"

"Hush, Golden Bamboo," said old Mung Ting. "I resent nothing, not even my exile, save for you. But in our home in Peking, so like a great palace filled with many servants, you possessed the riches of the world; here you sit in the bow of a fishing boat while your father spends many hours striving to catch the *samli* for the tables of the rich. There you were a fine lady; here you are just a maiden of little consequence, wearing a gown that will soon be ragged."

"It would mean nothing to me, O my father," replied Golden Bamboo, "that I possess no riches, if only you were happy and did not regret the lost power and grandeur which made you second in rank to the royal family."

"Power is so little, my daughter," he whispered, "that one word from one more powerful can destroy it all. It is only that my exile has taken from you the happy marriage which would have been yours at court."

"Who truly knows, august father? Perhaps even here on beautiful blue Hangchow I shall find greater happiness. Perhaps even here a bridegroom will come. There is joy even in hovels, if there be love."

"Who would send a matchmaker to the fisherman father of a maiden who has only beauty?" said Mung Ting. "Only the great may ask for you, my daughter, and the great do not ask for fishermen's daughters."

"Speak no more about it, august father," said

Golden Bamboo. "The sun is sinking behind the blue hills and night will come soon. Let us go to shore now with our catch."

Shortly thereafter, their boat tied up on shore, Mung Ting and Golden Bamboo walked along the shore toward their humble dwelling, which was so near the lake that the whispering of Hangchow's waves lulled them to sleep at night. Mung Ting's back was bowed under the weight of his catch, and many great blue-dotted silver *samli* glowed in the setting sun.

As they walked together they met a stranger who was very handsome. He was garbed as a laborer and he, too, bore a heavy burden on his back. His smile was gentle, his eyes honest. Golden Bamboo felt her heart move quickly when she looked into his eyes. The man bowed deeply to Mung Ting.

"Has this humble person permission to speak to the venerable stranger?" he asked.

Golden Bamboo knew she had never heard a man's voice so musical.

"What would you say to me?" asked Mung Ting gruffly, making to pass the young man.

"Only this: that it is the wish of this humble person to earn money for food and lodgings. Is it not possible that I too learn to fish for the silver *samli?"*

"It is indeed possible," replied Mung Ting, "for the lake is open to any who care to fish and the *samli* are not difficult to catch. I pray you, permit us to pass."

"If, then, we are to fish near each other in Hangchow," said the newcomer eagerly, "may we not speak as friends, sire? My name is Wu Fu—"

Mung Ting pressed past Wu Fu in anger. Golden Bamboo smiled at him in passing. Only when he had smiled back at her, did she remember that no maiden should look directly upon a young man's face, and bowed her dark head quickly in confusion, hiding the crimson which came to her cheeks.

Inside their dwelling on the lake shore she questioned her father.

"Why were you so gruff with this stranger Wu Fu? Perhaps he may be for us an omen of better fortune from this day on, for his name means 'five blessings.' "

"Five blessings or countless blessings," said Mung Ting in high anger, "he is a common laborer. Yet he dared to look upon you and to smile into your very eyes!"

"His smiles and his glances did not harm me, august father," began Golden Bamboo.

"Silence, my daughter!" said Mung Ting. "It is in my mind that you enjoyed his smiles and his glances, and I will never permit you to wed with one so lowly."

"Is it not, august father, too soon to speak of weddings?"

"Have I not bidden you to silence? Am I no longer your father to be obeyed?"

So Golden Bamboo spoke no further, but her heart was light and there was a little song on her lips. Her eyes danced with her thoughts, and her thoughts were with Wu Fu, who smiled so sweetly and whose voice was so like music.

Next day, and all the days after that, Wu Fu fished on Hangchow Lake, and always he managed that his boat should be close to the boat of Golden Bamboo and Mung Ting. Mung Ting spoke to him grudgingly and only when directly addressed, and when Wu Fu spoke to Golden Bamboo a frown would rest on the forehead of her father until the boats had drifted apart.

Wu Fu seemed never to catch many fish and never really to care. He was always happy and smiling.

"That young man is very shiftless and unworthy, my daughter," said Mung Ting many times. "He must catch *samli* for his living, yet he never is troubled if he catches not a single one. It is an evil thing for a man so young to take so little heed for the future."

One night Wu Fu came along the shore in the moonlight, and sat on the sand to play his flute. Inside the dwelling where Mung Ting and Golden Bamboo sat and held soft speech together, silence fell quickly. Wu Fu played on the flute like one long accustomed to such music. On her father's face Golden Bamboo could see how greatly he was puzzled, and worried, too. For young men who labored for their living were not masters of the flute.

Then Wu Fu ceased playing. Father and daughter listened, waiting for him to continue. He did begin again, but now he did not play the flute. Instead a golden voice went out through the night, singing softly,

"The storm is over.
    I see the clouds trailing past,
        Changing shape swiftly.
            A stream flows singing
                Under the little red bridge.

"Mysteriously the lotus leaves sway,
    When the breeze blows gently,

On their faces are the raindrops
Like beautiful soft pearls
Endlessly moving."

"Now indeed does Wu Fu become a young man of
strange mystery," said old Mung Ting, "for this song
he is singing is from the ancient Classics. How does it
transpire that the songs of the Classics come from the
lips of a poor man?"

"Please be silent, O august father," begged Golden
Bamboo, "for my heart takes joy in his singing, and
trembles with the music in his voice."

Mung Ting grumbled under his breath and fell
silent, while the voice of the singer drifted across the
waters of Hangchow.

"Today the sky is so blue,
Like the roofs of sacred temples.
The fragrance of jasmine flowers,
Is in my nostrils,
Sweet and soothing.

"In silver moonlight, beauty filled,
One should be so happy;
Yet I am sad,
And my heart is full
Of sorrow."

"It is in my heart, O my daughter," said old Mung Ting, "to forbid that you listen. For he sings the song called 'Solitude,' to tell you that he is alone, and he sings it close to our dwelling, knowing that you will hear and understand that he sings to you. I shall go and bid him depart at once."

"Pray let him continue," begged Golden Bamboo. And the plaintive song went on,

> "In the words of our ancient sage,
>   When one is fully happy,
>   One desires to cry.
>   For happiness becomes sadness,
>   Changing as the moon.

> "In the center of the sky,
>   I see thee, O Full Moon!
>   I am all alone.
>   I raise my little jade cup
>   Of wine to thee.

> "Dear Moon in the sky,
>   My beloved does not come,
>   And so I drink to thee,
>   I shall see my beloved
>   Again tomorrow."

The song ended and Golden Bamboo knew that Wu Fu had departed to his dwelling. Had he really sung for her? Was she his beloved? Was he alone and unhappy, when Golden Bamboo was not with him? Golden Bamboo's heart was happy because she believed herself his beloved; yet full of sorrow, too, knowing she might never wed one so lowly.

"O my father," she said to Mung Ting, "surely one who plays the flute so sweetly and sings so easily from the ancient Classics cannot truly be lowborn."

"If he is not lowborn," said Mung Ting, angered, "why should he hide in the clothing of a coolie and catch *samli* in Hangchow from under our very boat, thus taking food from our table, and money from our purse? This Wu Fu is a man of mystery and cannot be entirely honest."

But Golden Bamboo believed deeply in the goodness and honesty of Wu Fu, and determined to discover what she could of this young man whom she knew that she loved, so that her father might one day approve of him if ever he should send a matchmaker. He would send one, too, for had he not sung to her of love on the shores of Hangchow?

Next day Wu Fu smiled upon her as he had on all other days and spoke very politely to Mung

Ting. Mung Ting grunted in answer and turned his back, but all that Wu Fu did was smile. A young man must not become angry with an old man no matter how great his discourtesy. Golden Bamboo was mending a net, and her slender hands were moving swiftly and surely in their task while Wu Fu watched her. Suddenly he called out:

"Look, O august Mung Ting! Look, Golden Bamboo! See the boats which pass?"

Wu Fu held his boat beside the boat of Mung Ting while they turned their eyes toward the procession he had seen. There were two gaily decorated gunboats and a large house boat decorated with flags and streamers. The windows in the cabin were open, and delicate gauze curtains moved to and fro across them as the wind blew. Through one of the windows Golden Bamboo could see a beautifully dressed lady, with gorgeous headdress covered with flowers. Soft music came from somewhere in the procession, and with it the hum of conversation.

There were several boats all gaily decorated following the house boat—boats for the servants who hurried about, and a kitchen boat where food was prepared.

Wu Fu stood up in the bow of his boat, watching the procession go by, nodding his head and smiling

Golden Bamboo was mending a net.

while his eyes danced as though he were amused.

"Once," thought Golden Bamboo, "I lived like that, but for me all that glory is gone forever."

"Do you know who that is, Golden Bamboo?" asked Wu Fu. "It is the Governor of the Province who, with his entire family, is on the way to the Provincial capital. Is the procession not beautiful?"

Golden Bamboo scarcely heard his last words, for she had discovered a new mystery about Wu Fu.

"Tell me, Wu Fu," she said, "how it is that you knew who was in the house boat?"

"There is a banner on which are his name and rank. Did you not notice it at the stern of the house boat?"

"I saw it," replied Golden Bamboo, "and I wish you to tell me how it transpires that one who is but a laborer is yet able to read so easily and surely? Are you truly the laborer you seem, Wu Fu?"

"Would you be happy," said Wu Fu in a way she knew for a jest, "if you knew that I was someone of vast importance, perhaps even His Imperial Highness the Crown Prince, moving thus simply among his people that he might learn how they live and so be able to rule them better when he mounts the throne?"

"I would not care for you to be Crown Prince,"

said Golden Bamboo. "For me it is enough that you are simply Wu Fu."

Her face became all crimsoned with confusion as she realized whither her heart and her words were tending. She stopped, gasping, and lowered her eyes.

Wu Fu's voice was so low and tender that even Mung Ting, in the other end of the boat, could not hear.

"When I sang before your dwelling place, O little Golden Bamboo, I sang to you and thought of you, for you are my beloved! And my heart is filled with sorrow that I spoke just now in jest and that it is only Wu Fu who thus shows his heart to you—Wu Fu who loves you."

Her face was more crimson still but her eyes were filled with courage when she raised them.

"And I love you, Wu Fu!" she whispered. "My father must be persuaded that position and family do not matter, Wu Fu, but only that we so deeply love each other. Come tonight to our dwelling place and partake with us of our humble food!"

When Wu Fu came just before sunset to share the repast of Mung Ting and Golden Bamboo, the older man said little, but Golden Bamboo could see the little trouble-frown on his forehead and was afraid that he might forbid her to see Wu Fu again.

212

If he did, her heart would be utterly broken.

Golden Bamboo and Wu Fu were talking softly together, when there came suddenly the sound of a great commotion in the village, the pounding of many hoofs, horses ridden swiftly, servants shouting:

"Make way for the son of the governor! He rides through the village. Make way or be punished! Make way! Make way! Make way for His Eminence Huai Hsin!"

The head of a mounted cavalcade appeared. There were prancing curvetting little ponies of many colors, ponies from Outer Mongolia with long flowing manes. The outriders laid about them with whips.

"Make way for our young master, son of the governor!"

Mung Ting, Golden Bamboo and Wu Fu hurried to the gate which gave upon the street to watch the passing of the cavalcade.

"He makes a brave show, this son of the governor," said Wu Fu to Mung Ting.

"He is a bad man," replied Mung Ting, "and the people of Hangchow call him The Evil Star. It is better never to offend him, even by commenting upon him where others may hear and perhaps bear the story to him."

The cavalcade rode past and the last rider was garbed in all the glory of the sun; rich gown of satin and gold, a cap close fitting against the skull, with a feather drooping down the back and rising and falling with the prancing of his pony. The young man's eyes were black and arrogant and imperious. He was Huai Hsin.

As he rode past where the three watchers stood at the gate, his eyes fell upon the maiden. He pulled his pony to a walk and half turned toward the gate. His lips were twisted in a smile which caused Golden Bamboo's heart almost to stop beating with fear. The young man stared at her so boldly and halted so long there that already people were gathering to see what was the cause.

Mung Ting turned quickly to Golden Bamboo.

"Return to the house instantly, my daughter," he commanded.

Golden Bamboo turned and ran swiftly to the house, proof of her fear, since she never found reason for running.

The Evil Star stared for a moment, half smiling; but never once did he seem to see either old Mung Ting or young Wu Fu. Then the young man of the bold black eyes rode quickly on.

THE HONORABLE FIVE BLESSINGS

Mung Ting turned to Wu Fu.

"I am afraid, Wu Fu," he said simply.

"What is there to fear, O Mung Ting?" asked Wu Fu.

"This profligate Huai Hsin has looked upon the beauty of Golden Bamboo, and I am afraid. For in this city he sends for maidens whose faces please him, and the maidens go because their fathers are afraid to say no to a governor's son. They know that whatever The Evil Star does, his father the governor believes is right that he do."

"Let there be no cause for worry, venerable Mung Ting," said Wu Fu. "I shall help you to protect Golden Bamboo."

"How can you help, Wu Fu?" snapped Mung Ting. "You are but a coolie whom The Evil Star will brush aside."

And even while they talked there, two men came riding back down the street from the direction whence The Evil Star had vanished. They were proud and arrogant and wasted no words as they spoke to Mung Ting.

"Our young master bids us come here, old fisherman," they told him, "to take your daughter to him! She is to go with us at once, and tomorrow, if the young master is pleased with her, he will send you a gift of gold."

"Does the young master send you as matchmakers, seeking the hand of my daughter in marriage?" asked Mung Ting.

Together and loudly the two men laughed.

"Be not a fool, old one!" said one. "Does the son of a governor choose a fisherman's daughter for his bride? Let there be no talk of marriage! Give the maiden into our hands and be happy that our young master does not have your head for asking foolish questions!"

"She will not go with you," said Mung Ting quickly. "She is my daughter. She remains with me. Sooner would I sink her in the depths of Hangchow Lake than give her into the hands of one so vile as The Evil Star!"

"Take heed for yourself, old man!" said one. "For our young master will have you decapitated for your defiance."

"He may do so, but ere I die my daughter will die at my hands or her own!"

"So be it, then, old fool!" they said. "We return at once to take your words to our young master."

They rode away, and when they came back quickly a short time later, there were others with them, and riding in the midst of them The Evil Star himself, his face all black with a frown of fury. He quickly dismounted and with his servants around him stepped through the gate into the courtyard of Mung Ting.

"What does here the son of the governor?" asked Mung Ting bravely.

"Out of my pathway, old one!" said the Evil Star. "Your daughter has pleased my fancy. I have come for her."

Trembling, fearful, choking back the sobs in her throat, Golden Bamboo heard all from behind the shutters of her window. Ere The Evil Star should take her she would strangle herself with some cord. She looked about for one that would suffice, while her ears strained to catch every word which passed at the gate.

"Golden Bamboo is not for any man as evil as Huai Hsin," said Wu Fu to The Evil Star softly. "She is not for any man, save after the usual custom, when a matchmaker is sent and a marriage arranged."

The Evil Star laughed.

"The son of a governor does not wed with a mere—"

What The Evil Star might have said will never be known, for suddenly the slim strong left hand of Wu Fu went forth and grasped the queue of the governor's son. When he had grasped it firmly, and so quickly none had really seen him do it, Wu Fu pulled suddenly, so that the angry face of The Evil Star was quite close to his own. Then Wu Fu lifted his right hand even more quickly than he had lifted his left, and struck The Evil Star across the cheek. So hard was the blow that the feet of Huai Hsin refused to hold him and he fell, striking his head against a cobblestone.

Shouts of great anger rose up from The Evil Star's servants. A crowd of people gathered in the street. The Evil Star rose, his face flaming, his hand covering the mark on his cheek which was shaped like the hand of Wu Fu. In his fury The Evil Star had forgotten Golden Bamboo.

"Seize this upstart!" cried The Evil Star. "Take him straightway to the magistrate, where I shall bear witness against him. Your head shall fall within the hour, fool! You dare to strike the governor's son?"

"I dare to strike him," said Wu Fu, just as softly as before, "and I shall strike him again unless he steps outside the gate of the venerable Mung Ting!"

And since Wu Fu raised his hand as he spoke, The Evil Star hastily stepped back into the street. His servants immediately surrounded Wu Fu and made him prisoner.

From behind her shutters Golden Bamboo watched them take away as prisoner the man who held all the love of her heart. She knew that he was being led away to bend his neck under the beheading knife. When he was out of sight she raced forth to her father.

"It is an evil day, O my daughter," he told her, "that The Evil Star gazed upon your beauty. For he will destroy Wu Fu."

Golden Bamboo wrung her slender white hands.

"Is there nothing we may do, O my father? Is there no sacrifice we may make to save him? O my father, if Wu Fu is slain I shall destroy myself. Make haste then and see what may be done!"

"I shall go to the magistrate, Golden Bamboo," said her father, "and say what I may be allowed to say. But I am no longer a powerful official and I do not believe my words will have weight. Do you—my daughter—go into the dwelling place and hide until I return."

Mung Ting shuffled quickly down the street toward the *yamen* of the magistrate, while Golden Bamboo watched him go. Then, because her father had so bidden her, and she must obey, she went into the house, but she came out again at once and listened to the words of the people who had gathered in a crowd outside the gate.

"Wu Fu will surely be decapitated!" said one.

"The Evil Star will have his will of Golden Bamboo!" said another, "after he has destroyed Wu Fu and old Mung Ting."

"If only something could be done to this Evil Star," said another, "so that he take no more of our maidens into his palace by force!"

Meanwhile Wu Fu was led to the *yamen* of the magistrate, who came quickly in all his official robes when word went to him that the governor's son waited upon him with a prisoner to be judged.

The magistrate presented himself, bowing low to the arrogant Evil Star.

"Where then is the prisoner?" he asked of The Evil Star with the greatest politeness.

The Evil Star pointed at Wu Fu.

"What has he done?" asked the magistrate.

"What does it matter what he has done?" cried The Evil Star. "Is it not enough that I, Huai Hsin, bring him here to be judged? Mete out punishment, then! Send him away to be decapitated!"

Trembling and afraid before the arrogant young man, the magistrate turned his eyes upon Wu Fu.

"You are a prisoner, son of many turtles!" he cried.

"Do you not know that it is the law that a prisoner must kneel to be judged? Why then do you not kneel?"

"I kneel to no living man in all the Middle Kingdom, save one, His Majesty the Emperor," said Wu Fu quietly. "It is for you, and this foolish young man, and all of you, to kneel to *me!*"

"What is this treason?" cried the magistrate.

"What is this evil felony?" cried The Evil Star. "Who is this upstart who says so calmly that a son of a governor should kneel at his feet? Bid that his head be stricken from his shoulders, O magistrate, so that I may continue on my way when justice has been meted out. And is it not law that when one is guilty of such high treason, all his family must die with him?"

"It is the law, O Evil Star," said Wu Fu calmly, before the magistrate could make answer, "that the tiger must be destroyed with the cub, the root with the branch, and it is my wish, before you kneel at my feet as I have bidden you, that you remember well this law!"

In spite of the fact that Wu Fu wore the poor garments of a fisherman, in spite of the fact that he seemed a coolie, the magistrate hesitated and there was something of doubt in the face of The Evil Star.

For the language of Wu Fu was the language of a man who had long and faithfully studied the Classics. None noted that the aged Mung Ting had entered and was listening.

"Who are you?" demanded the magistrate.

"Does there not dwell in this village an aged retired gentleman known as Wen Tung Ho?" asked Wu Fu. "Send for him then, that he may tell you who I am."

"Wen Tung Ho?" said The Evil Star. "Who are you who sends for Wen Tung Ho as though he were a common man? Wen Tung Ho was once a great man at court!"

But Mung Ting, feeling that none would be sent to Wen Tung Ho, himself hurried from the *yamen,* traveling faster than his old legs had carried him for many years. When he finally persuaded the aged Wen Tung Ho to return with him to the *yamen* they were in time, for the magistrate had not yet pronounced judgment upon Wu Fu.

"From my heart I give thanks that you bring Wen Tung Ho," said Wu Fu, to Mung Ting as the two old men entered together.

Wen Tung Ho, old and stooped and tottering with the weight of years, lifted his head eagerly as Wu Fu spoke.

"Who is this man," he asked in a cracked old voice, "who speaks with a voice which these old ears so well remember? Let me come close to him that I may see, for my eyes are no longer young and I see but little save such things as are very near."

Mung Ting led Wen Tung Ho to stand before Wu Fu.

"Do you recognize me, O Wen Tung Ho?" asked Wu Fu.

Wen Tung Ho trembled.

"For many years I taught you," he said in a voice that shook almost as though the old man wept, "and I know every line of your face, every tone of your golden voice. Kneel, O magistrate! Kneel all you who hear my voice, and kowtow thrice and thrice and thrice, to His Imperial Highness, the Crown Prince of the Kingdom of Yuan, which is in Peking! He is the son of the Emperor!"

Aghast the magistrate stood, and The Evil Star.

"It is in our heart," said Wu Fu, "to remind you, son of a governor, that where there is treason against the ruler the tiger must be destroyed with the cub, the root with the branch. It is our decree then that you and your father and all your family be banished forever from the Middle Kingdom! Kneel to receive sentence at our hands!"

But before any of the frightened ones could kneel to the Prince, a breathless sobbing maiden entered the *yamen* running, to fling herself at the feet of The Evil Star.

"Spare him, O Great One!" cried Golden Bamboo. "Spare Wu Fu! Take my life in his stead; take me into your palace if you will it. For his freedom I give myself into your hands. But I beseech you, allow Wu Fu to go free!"

For a moment silence held sway in the *yamen*.

The smile, the eyes, the lips of Wu Fu were very gentle as he looked down upon Golden Bamboo who would make so great a sacrifice for one whom she knew merely as Wu Fu, a fisherman. Then he turned to the others and his expression changed.

"We await the bended knee!" he said.

And all knelt quickly to kowtow to the Crown Prince. The Evil Star knelt too, moaning, begging for forgiveness and mercy.

Her eyes very wide and frightened, Golden Bamboo looked into the face of Wu Fu as he bent to lift her to her feet—while all the others there struck their heads abjectly against the cobblestones in the ancient kowtow.

"Who are you, O Wu Fu?" whispered Golden Bamboo. "Who are you that all the great ones bend the knee to you in kowtow?"

"I am Wu Fu who loves you, little Golden Bamboo, I am Wu Fu who loves you beyond all words to say. And Wu Fu is the Crown Prince of whom he spoke jestingly."

Suddenly Wu Fu knelt at the feet of Golden Bamboo.

"In the name of His Imperial Majesty our father, whom we shall one day succeed on the throne of Yuan, O Golden Bamboo," said Wu Fu, "we place all that kingdom most humbly at the hem of your gown!"

SINGING KITES OF TAI SHAN

SINGING KITES OF TAI SHAN

EACH BLOSSOM walked softly upon her bound feet, careful not to waken her little mistress. Over a charcoal burner from which rose the faintest wisps of blue smoke, she held the delicate garments of Snow Coral, warming them for the moment when her mistress would rise and don them. Peach Blossom shivered, for in spite of the heat from the huge charcoal burner, the room was cold.

Tiger and leopard skins covered the floor. Two delicate peonies in a green jade vase stood on Snow Coral's dressing table. Several sachet bags hung from the carved posts of the beautiful bed, and their perfume filled the sleeping chamber. The half-drawn bed curtains of pink silk swayed slightly, and this little movement told Peach Blossom that her mistress had wakened. Approaching the bed she bowed deeply, offering the traditional genuflections.

"May peace and happiness greet you this lovely morning, O precious Snow Coral," she said.

"Is it my faithful Peach Blossom?" came the musical voice of Snow Coral. "I was not sure that I had wakened when I heard your footfall. I have been dreaming and my dream was fearful."

"Dreams are not real. Forget them and smile, for the garden today is gorgeous under its white mantle of snow. The trees and bushes are heavily laden with its fluffy whiteness."

"I am still frightened, Peach Blossom. My dreams were horrible."

Peach Blossom was superstitious, but she tried to hide her fear when the beloved Snow Coral spoke of terrible dreams.

"What was this dream, O Snow Coral?" she asked. Her mistress grew pale.

"Do not ask me to speak of it." she shuddered. "I fear it portends some evil thing."

"It was only a dream, after all, Snow Coral," comforted Peach Blossom.

"Only a dream, that is true, but last night was the second night I dreamed it."

This indeed was an evil portent! Peach Blossom turned her face away so that her mistress should not see how it was filled with fear.

Snow Coral rose gracefully from her bed and moved to the window. She peered dreamily out toward China's oldest sacred mountain, Tai Shan, the burial place of the Great Sage, Confucius. It rose upward to the height of three *li,* all its marvelous symmetry cloaked now in snow.

"Tai Shan is more beautiful than ever," said Snow Coral. "The whole countryside is gorgeous under the snow. But I am sorry that we shall be unable to fly our musical kite this cold morning."

Peach Blossom was disappointed, too, for she well knew how thoroughly Snow Coral enjoyed the pastime of kite flying. Besides, her kite was a marvelous creation, and there was not another one like it in Tianfu.

Slowly Snow Coral donned the clothing Peach Blossom had warmed over the charcoal burner, and sought comfort for her numbed fingers at the fire. Her eyes were wistful as she looked out over the beautiful white mantled garden. Snow Coral was not happy. She seldom was happy and Peach Blossom understood why.

"It is thought of Tong Shih which makes my little mistress unhappy," she said suddenly. "I wish your father, General Chu, had refused to hearken to the words of sly matchmakers after your dear mother ascended the Dragon Throne on High."

"Hush, Peach Blossom, you must not be disloyal. My father did right to give me a stepmother, for he had no son to worship at his grave and it was necessary that he wed again. It would not be right for the name of Chu to vanish from the land. It is our duty to be loyal to my father. In accordance with the custom of filial piety I must do everything possible to please my father, and how better can I please him than by being pleasant to my stepmother, Tong Shih?"

"But should she not also be pleasant to her daughter?" asked Peach Blossom with anger. "I know that she hates you. She would feel happier, my Snow Coral, if you were far away, even if you were dead!"

"You must not speak thus!" said Snow Coral, raising her voice. "It is an evil thing to say of my stepmother."

"I shall say on because I know I speak truly," insisted Peach Blossom. "The family of Tong Shih is a wicked family, full of many schemes. They covet the vast riches of General Chu, which can never be theirs if the general dies while you still live."

"Hush, Peach Blossom, I will not permit you to speak further in this manner."

Peach Blossom subsided, but she murmured continually to herself as she went about her manifold duties. Now and again she looked at Snow Coral, who stood drooping at the window, and in her black eyes there was a world of love for her mistress. Who, she thought, could have helped loving her? She was so gracefully slender. Her lips were a scarlet bow; her white hands so soft and fragile. Her hair was black and so abundant that when it came down it was as though an ebon cloud had swept in through the window. Her feet were so tiny they would scarcely have filled her own small cupped hands. She was like a figure done in the rarest jade by the greatest genius among China's craftsmen.

To her mistress Peach Blossom was more friend and companion than *amah,* and fear of what Snow Coral's dream might mean had caused her to speak more freely than she had ever dared speak before.

Soon Tong Shih, stern and unsmiling of face, came to speak with Snow Coral, and, as always when she gazed upon the maiden, her eyes seemed filled with anger.

"You have slept late again, Snow Coral!" she said harshly. "I shall tell General Chu that his daughter is lazy; that she sleeps when she should be reading the Classics or the poetry of Li Po. How can the servants enter your room to make it orderly when you are forever in the way?"

"I am sorry, O Tong Shih," said Snow Coral, her eyes filled with unhappiness, "but I slept no later today than yesterday or the day before that. And if my father were here he would not feel that his daughter, whom he loves, should make haste to save the servants labor or trouble. They are well paid and I am sure that they do not feel themselves injured."

"You would criticize the words of your mother?" snapped Tong Shih. "You are an ungrateful daughter and it would not surprise me if your beauty changed to ugliness because of the disloyal thoughts of your heart. Why do you not do something? Even if you flew your kite, foolish as it seems to me for one who could do much that is really useful, you would at least free the house of your troublesome presence."

"It is cold in the garden, O Tong Shih," protested Snow Coral.

" 'It is cold in the garden'!" mimicked Tong Shih. "You are so fragile then that a little snow may do you harm, Snow Coral?"

The maiden turned and spoke to Peach Blossom, who was standing stiff and straight as she looked at Tong Shih and seemed ready to speak rude words to her any moment.

"Bring my heavy garments, Peach Blossom," she said quietly, "and we will go into the garden to fly my kite. Perhaps the sun will come out soon and it will be warmer."

A few minutes later two figures, so heavily bundled in furs that they seemed twice as big as they really were, went into the garden. Peach Blossom brushed the soft snow from one of the benches under the snow-

covered trees and placed on the cleared space several
pillows she had first warmed over the charcoal burner.
Snow Coral sat down while Peach Blossom arranged
the kite, first making sure that a smaller charcoal
burner rested close and warm against the tiny feet of
her mistress.

Now Peach Blossom gave into the fur-mittened
hands of Snow Coral the string of the butterfly kite.
The maiden smiled suddenly with reawakened happiness, for she was proud of this kite and took great
joy in flying it. It was shaped like a gorgeous butterfly,
and across the tips of the bow in its center was stretched
a silken cord, made stiff and taut with glue, so that it
was like the string of some musical instrument. Even
as Peach Blossom held the kite, and before she allowed
it to fly free, the wind blowing across the snowy garden
caressed the little string, which hummed softly as
though it too were happy.

From wing-tip to wing-tip, from head to tail, the
kite was a perfectly fashioned butterfly. Even the eyes
were lifelike, but they were little drumheads of skin,
and just above them tiny drumsticks were fastened to
the head of the butterfly, held in place so that they
could swing in but one direction, and when the kite
flew they struck against the eyes and made soft drum-
ming music. The wing-tips of the butterfly were hung

with bells so small one could scarcely see them, yet so strong was their tinkling that even when the kite was high in the cloudless sky people on the ground below could hear their soft chiming.

Peach Blossom released the kite, which went soaring away, out over the snow-capped wall of the garden, out over the garden of the deserted dwelling place next door, and so on—out—as far as the string would reach, until the kite grew small and looked like a butterfly indeed, against the white mantle of snow which covered sacred Tai Shan. Peach Blossom smiled as she noted the happiness in the eyes of Snow Coral.

But Peach Blossom's superstitions kept turning her thoughts to Snow Coral's dream of last night. And she was afraid of something else, too, of which she was reminded now because the kite had flown out across the neighboring garden. That might be an evil omen, for lately Peach Blossom had heard fearful whispers about the adjoining garden—that it was thought to be haunted; that after nightfall ghosts and fairies walked silently through the garden and the huge house, empty for so many years.

With all her heart Peach Blossom wished that General Chu, gone on a long journey to attend to official matters for the Emperor, were home again.

236

SINGING KITES OF TAI SHAN

Into another Shantung garden had recently come Kung Hao, a direct descendant of Confucius. His father was Governor of the Province of Chihli, where Kung Hao had been born. Now that Kung Hao was old enough to think of becoming an official in the government service, his father had sent him back to their vast estates in Shantung to study and to meditate. And with him he sent his grim-faced servant, Ta Liu. Ta Liu was seven feet eight inches tall! Governor Kung had found this giant of lowly birth years before in a famine district and had bought him as a present for his son Kung Hao. Ta Liu had been happy in his servitude to Kung Hao, whom he loved and worshiped.

And Kung Hao in his turn regarded the giant as a friend and companion. He was happy that the big man had come to live with him in the house of many rooms and the huge garden filled with many tablets to remind him of Confucius, his greatest ancestor. Often he read them to Ta Liu, who could not read wise words of the sage inscribed on these tablets and thought it a miracle that the characters his master studied meant words.

Kung Hao felt he should apply himself to be worthy of his august ancestry, and so spent most of his time at his studies in the garden, which was a haven

of peace and a great inspiration, for near here had
Confucius studied and meditated, and Kung Hao was
sure that his spirit still hovered over the old place.

Today, though snow lay lightly on the garden, they
walked as usual. Kung Hao in a gown of sky blue,
bordered with gold, and with a girdle of gold clasped
by a golden buckle that was set with gleaming precious
stones. His cap was of black velvet, topped by a pearl
button of great beauty.

"I shall read to you today from the inscriptions, Ta
Liu," said Kung Hao in his musical voice. "You shall
walk close behind me to push the snow from the tablets
when I tell you!"

Ta Liu looked far down upon his handsome proud
young master and smiled very widely.

"Whatever is your wish, O Kung Hao, that is the
law of Ta Liu, who never tires of listening."

So they walked and Kung Hao read softly:

" 'Mutual confidence is the invisible thread which
binds men together as friends.' "

Ta Liu nodded wisely, understanding nothing, but
knowing it could do no harm to seem wise.

" 'When out of doors behave as though you were
entertaining a distinguished guest. In ruling the people behave as though you were officiating at a solemn
sacrifice. What you would not want done to yourself,

238

do not unto others. In public as in private life, you will excite no ill will.' "

Ta Liu nodded again.

Suddenly Kung Hao stopped.

"I hear soft music," he said, "and it seems to come from the air above our heads!"

Ta Liu smiled delightedly.

"Spring will soon be here, O my master," he said, "and though the snow still covers Tai Shan many people are flying their kites today. That music comes from one of them. Great skill was required in the making of that kite which makes such music, and for a long time I have been trying to decide which of the many kites now flying causes the sounds."

"I had hoped," said Kung Hao severely yet with a twinkle in his eyes, "that you were listening to my reading of the tablets instead of the music of a singing kite."

"I bow my head in contrition," said Ta Liu, "for I am indeed sorry. I should lose my head for allowing my rapt attention to waver. But are not the kites beautiful? Especially that gorgeous kite which is shaped like a butterfly. I wonder whence it is flying. My eyes are not strong enough to follow the string."

"Nor are your ears sharp enough," said Kung Hao, "for it is the butterfly kite which makes the music, and the string from which it flies disappears into the garden of our next door neighbor. I should like, O Ta Liu, to possess a kite exactly like that one!"

"That is possible, young master, for once I was a maker of kites and I know exactly what materials to use in fashioning a butterfly kite that will also make music. I go at once to begin my labors."

Many days had passed since that cold morning when Tong Shih had sent Snow Coral out in the garden to fly the butterfly kite. General Chu had not yet returned, but word had come that he was en route, and as the days passed Tong Shih became ever more harsh toward Snow Coral, who went out now without being bidden, no matter how cold the garden, to fly her kite.

On this fateful morning the kite sped out swiftly. The little drumsticks pounded merrily; the bells tinkled; the wind played a tune across the silken cord —and Snow Coral tried not to think that last night she had dreamed for the third time her dream of dread.

Snow Coral tried to forget the dream as the musical kite played out with a vast humming of string. But when the big butterfly had reached the string's end, and again floated back and forth across the face of Tai Shan, she bowed her head in sorrowful thought, while

Peach Blossom watched the kite with childish pleasure.

Snow Coral raised her head at last, wearily, and looked toward the kite.

"Peach Blossom!" she cried. "Peach Blossom, what is happening? Our kite is falling! It will be dashed to pieces."

"No, Snow Coral," answered Peach Blossom, "it is not falling."

"But it flies much lower than usual!"

"Our kite rides in its usual place," said Peach Blossom. "If you will look closely you will see that the kite which flies lower is another kite, though exactly like ours!"

Instantly Snow Coral forgot her dream.

"Who in all Tianfu," she asked angrily, "dares copy a kite belonging to Snow Coral? See if your eyes can follow the string, Peach Blossom. If we can find this person who has made a kite like ours I shall tell my father when he comes, so that he may punish him!"

"I have already followed the string, O Snow Coral," said Peach Blossom, "but I feared to speak because it comes from the garden next door, which everyone knows is haunted. The kite is therefore a ghost kite, on a ghost string!"

"I do not believe in ghost kites and ghost strings, or even in ghost people," said Snow Coral. "Do you climb the rockery at once and see who dares be so bold as to copy my kite!"

Peach Blossom climbed quickly to the top of the rockery, while Snow Coral waited below. The serving maid looked over into the next garden, screamed suddenly, and came down from the rockery so fast she almost fell.

"I saw two ghosts over there, O Snow Coral," she gasped. "One was small, but the other was over ten feet tall! And these ghosts fly the second butterfly kite."

Snow Coral hesitated. She didn't believe in ghosts, but if the people in the next garden *were* ghosts, she would not be violating the rules of maidenly propriety by climbing the rockery and looking at them. So she bade Peach Blossom climb again and help her up. Side by side they looked into the adjoining garden, while Peach Blossom called out boldly:

"Are you ghosts or mortals?"

At this sudden query Ta Liu and Kung Hao laughed aloud, which so angered Peach Blossom that for a moment she could find nothing further to say, and so abashed Snow Coral that she climbed down the rockery without waiting for a reply.

Kung Hao sobered instantly and made courteous answer.

"We are only mortals," he said. "I am Kung Hao and this is my servant Ta Liu. What do you wish of me?"

"How comes that kite in your possession?" asked Peach Blossom, pointing to the one which flew so low. "Where did you procure one so exactly like the butterfly kite of my mistress? She has seen it and it has made her exceedingly angry."

At once Kung Hao, who had caught so brief a glimpse of Snow Coral, but that glimpse enough to make his heart dance swiftly in his breast, was all contrition.

"Ta Liu made it for me," he said. "I am grieved to learn that it has offended your honorable mistress. Is there aught I can do to make amends?"

"I do not know, for just now my mistress is angered."

"Please tell your mistress that I send my humble respects and many genuflections and will most happily accept any penalty she may wish to exact for my unspeakable impertinence. My kite having offended her, I shall order my servant to destroy it at once. Please say to your mistress that I would offer my humblest apologies, my deepest genuflections, to her in person, else I cannot pursue my studies in peace."

Below the rockery Snow Coral heard every word, and her heart moved faster when she thought of meet-

ing the handsome young man of whom she had caught
a fleeting glimpse from the rockery. She remembered
that Governor Kung of Chihli, to whom this estate
belonged, had a son called Kung Hao, of whom he had
proudly spoken when he had once exchanged official
visits with General Chu. Perhaps that visit of long ago
would justify this violation of the proprieties?

"I heard all he said," whispered Snow Coral to
Peach Blossom. "I should like to accept his apology
myself. Do you think it would be immodest for me to
do so?"

Peach Blossom replied softly:

"He appears a very honest person and he has a wonderful smile. I like him. I think this once we might
defy convention, for I am with you—and besides, I
should like to see closer that huge servant of his."

Snow Coral climbed again to the top of the rockery.
Immediately Kung Hao addressed her, bowing deeply
as he did so.

"Kung Hao extends to your august self his humblest
apologies, and knows that he does not deserve to gaze
upon your gold and jade person. He will at once command his servant to destroy the kite. Or may he present
it to your august delectable self?"

Snow Coral flushed deeply and prettily and for a
moment could not find words to answer.

"I accept your apology," she said, "but cannot think of accepting your kite. Please keep it and do not destroy it. I find we are not strangers after all. I am Snow Coral, daughter of General Chu, and years ago our fathers exchanged cards in token of everlasting friendship. Pray do not allow what has happened to disturb your studies. Farewell!"

And Snow Coral vanished from the rockery, leaving Kung Hao all at once feeling as though the sun had stopped shining. He could not think at all of his studies. He could think only of Snow Coral's fragile beauty, could hear only the music of her voice.

"Ta Liu," he said at last, "it is my wish to know better this gorgeous daughter of General Chu, my father's friend. Soon I shall be leaving Shantung. I have seen Snow Coral but once, but if I were never to see her again I feel I should die."

Ta Liu smiled widely.

"It is a grave matter to be of high birth," he said sagely. "For those who are people of distinction, the rules are very hard to break. For the lowly they are not difficult at all, which now seems fortunate—since the *amah* of Snow Coral, that Peach Blossom, did not look upon me with entire disfavor. Tonight I shall contrive to meet her in her mistress's garden, and I shall be disloyal indeed to my master, O Kung Hao, if I do

245

not prevail upon Peach Blossom to persuade the marvelous Snow Coral to meet my master again—perhaps in that selfsame garden, when the moon is high?"

" 'A young girl's voice should be as the song of the oriole or the twittering of a thrush,' " said Kung Hao softly. "Now I understand what those words mean. If only you can arrange it, Ta Liu!"

So wisely and well did Ta Liu strive for his master, and so greatly did Peach Blossom wish happiness for Snow Coral, that, the second night thereafter, when the moon was a silver lamp in the sky, Kung Hao came over the high wall and met Snow Coral in the garden of her father's estate.

They sat on a marble bench under an immense spreading tree. The night was utterly still. One could hear the leaves of the weeping willow caress the waters of the goldfish pond as the wind stirred them sleepily.

As they sat, the hands of Kung Hao captured the hands of Snow Coral and held them in a gentle clasp. They gazed timidly into each other's eyes but for a moment neither could find a word of speech. Then Snow Coral, trembling, smiled.

"Do you think me unmaidenly, O Kung Hao?" she asked.

Instantly he made reply.

"Your face has been before me since I first saw you.

Your image has been always in my heart. How then could you be unmaidenly in my eyes? That you may know my feelings I must tell you with my first words that I seek your hand in marriage and pray that you find me not unworthy. I crave a sign from you—as a token that I may find favor in your eyes. I beg you to press my hands with your fingers."

Snow Coral lowered her head in quick amazed confusion, but her hands pressed his as he had suggested. Kung Hao immediately stood and placed his hands gently on the shoulders of his beloved.

"Beyond all words to express, you have made me happy," he said softly. "For I knew when I saw you on the rockery that I loved you and would always love you. It is the dearest wish of my heart that our fathers give their consent and that I may send the matchmaker. And now I would not leave you, but it is unwise for me to linger when someone may discover us and make it impossible for us ever to be happy. In two days I shall go to my father in Chihli to arrange for our marriage. But tomorrow night, O my beloved, will you not come into my garden and walk with me, while I read to you from the tablets of my great ancestor Confucius? I must see you again before I go to tell my father, and in my garden there is none to hear or carry tales."

Snow Coral walked with him, hand in hand, to the wall. As he clambered up he turned and said softly:

"May we be together when our hair becomes silver, and may our happiness be eternal."

Then he was gone and Snow Coral returned quietly to the house, never dreaming that evil fortune had sent Tong Shih into the garden this night of all nights, and that her stepmother had seen all, had heard every word that had passed between Snow Coral and Kung Hao.

Fortune had favored Tong Shih. The marriage might have been arranged before she had suspected, but for her good luck. Now she was warned and could make her plans. In the privacy of her own chambers she smiled evilly to herself, and sent a trusted servant for certain members of her greedy family.

Next evening Kung Hao and Snow Coral walked long and talked much in the garden of the Kungs. They were happy beyond happiness as they planned their future with hearts light with utter joy. Ta Liu and Peach Blossom stood guard, but none thought of danger which might threaten from the garden of Tong Shih.

"Tomorrow morning early I depart to hold speech with my father," whispered Kung Hao, "but I leave Ta Liu behind me to see that no harm befalls you,

248

Snow Coral, my beloved!"

It was late when Snow Coral and Peach Blossom climbed over the wall and went to their rooms, thinking themselves undiscovered. Tong Shih was very shrewd and did nothing at all until she was sure Kung Hao had departed from Tianfu. Then she sent for Snow Coral. The maiden came, and found Tong Shih surrounded by members of her own unpleasant family.

"You have disgraced the name of Chu," Tong Shih said grimly. "All these people witnessed with me that you spent many hours last night in the garden of the Kungs. Your father would die of shame and Governor Kung would lose his governorship if the people of Tianfu should hear even a whisper of this. 'The great Kung, descendant of Confucius, has a son who meets secretly in a garden an unmarried maiden!' Thus will they speak—and all the fault is yours."

Snow Coral's heart seemed to turn to stone in her breast for she realized how surely Tong Shih had trapped her. None in all the land would believe the garden visit innocent. All would think of it, and speak of it loudly, as a bitter disgrace. Tong Shih smiled a little, grimly, as she seemed to read the mind of Snow Coral, saw her face whiten, and her fragile hands go to her fluttering breast.

"I understand your words, O Tong Shih," said Snow

249

Coral bitterly. "I know that in your heart you realize that I am innocent of any wrongdoing; but I know, too, the ancient customs and what this disgrace would mean to my father, to Governor Kung and to Kung Hao, whom I love with all my heart. I am in your power. I understand you have a plan. Tell me what it is."

Tong Shih hesitated, her thin, cruel nostrils quivering. She looked at her relatives for support and all of them nodded. Then she turned back to Snow Coral.

"You will wed the Tutelary God!" she said.

Snow Coral's face blanched.

"But a maiden weds the Tutelary God only when she is about to die!" she gasped, her eyes wide with terror.

Tong Shih went on inexorably:

"The story will go forth that you are extremely ill. The day for the wedding to the Tutelary God will be set immediately for two days hence—"

"But I am *not* ill, Tong Shih! I am strong and well."

Desperately Snow Coral fought for time to think—pretending not to understand—although her stepmother's plot was all too clear.

"There is but one way that you can avert dishonor," said Tong Shih grimly, "with a knife! Decide quickly —or my relatives will go out at once to spread the story of your shame in the garden of the Kungs."

Snow Coral realized that her case was hopeless and bowed her head in defeat. As she slowly left the room, Tong Shih smiled—a smile that was gloating and infinitely evil.

In her own room, knowing now that all the servants were on watch over her lest she strive to escape, Snow Coral flung herself weeping into the arms of Peach Blossom, who held her and rocked her to and fro as though she had been a baby.

"And so for a little hour of happiness I must pay with my life. Now I understand my dream of evil portent."

Peach Blossom paused for a moment in rocking Snow Coral to and fro. A thought had come to her. Perhaps Ta Liu might help her with a plan; but, no matter what they did, it must be done with the greatest secrecy. Tong Shih's power in the house of Chu was now absolute; all she had to do was speak a word to bring disgrace upon a proud name, and Snow Coral was giving up her life to prevent that dishonor. Yes, Peach Blossom must be very careful.

So that day the word went forth in Tianfu that Snow Coral had fallen desperately ill and would die; that she was to be married to the Tutelary God the very next day, before she grew too weak to endure the

251

ceremony of bridal.

After the moon rose, Peach Blossom slipped quietly into the garden of the Kungs and talked long and earnestly with Ta Liu the giant servant of Kung Hao.

"If they were to marry," said Ta Liu at last, "then what could people say about them? How then would it serve this evil Tong Shih to tell lying tales about your mistress and my master?"

"But how could that be managed?" said Peach Blossom, weeping. "Your master is gone and will be away for some time. His father and the father of my mistress would have to be consulted first, and Snow Coral weds the Tutelary God tomorrow."

"I shall send a friend whom I can trust to overtake Kung Hao," said Ta Liu. "He should catch him before he reaches Chefoo, and into his ears he will whisper the words that I tell him."

"And those words, Ta Liu?"

"That my master in turn is to send forth messages, one to his father, the Governor of Chihli and one to General Chu. The message to General Chu will say that his good friend Governor Kung desires to meet him in Chefoo to discuss a matter of vast importance. The message to Governor Kung will simply ask him to meet his son in Chefoo. When the two men arrive in Chefoo and are met by Kung Hao, my master will explain everything."

"But how foolish is all this! How shall it profit my mistress that her father and your master's father meet with her beloved in Chefoo, so many *li* distant from Tai Shan?"

"It shall profit this: that Kung Hao shall tell each of them that he wishes the hand of Snow Coral in marriage. He is a very wise young man, my master, and will without doubt persuade them both that it is the best match that could possibly be made."

"Still it seems idle talk to my ears," said Peach Blossom impatiently. "Almost as silly as though we spoke of our own wedding, in Chefoo."

"That also," said Ta Liu grinning suddenly, "may be a matter for later discussion."

"And meanwhile, my little mistress, most precious of all living maidens, weds tomorrow with the Tutelary God of Tianfu! We *must* prevent that marriage."

"We are weak," said Ta Liu, "and they are strong. We are few and they are many. We are stupid and they are wise. There is nothing we can do to stop the marriage of Snow Coral to the Tutelary God. So the ceremony must take place."

"So you make mock of me, you stupid coolie giant!" stormed Peach Blossom. "You speak of foolish plans only to spend more time with me, while in the house

253

my little mistress weeps her heart away. I feared always there was nothing that could be done. You but confirm this fear, O speaker of empty words!"

Peach Blossom tried her best to strike Ta Liu across the face with her hand, but even though she stood on her toes she could not reach his face. The giant smiled at her rage, placed his huge hand on her head, bade her return to her mistress, say nothing, and trust to Ta Liu—for had not Kung Hao left him behind to watch over the safety of Snow Coral?

The faces of Snow Coral and Peach Blossom were wooden of expression because they had resigned themselves to the grim wedding ceremony. Word had come to the home of the Chus that the Tutelary God had been placed in readiness to receive his bride, and Tong Shih had issued her last grim instructions. Prepared as though she were ill unto death, Snow Coral, her face as white as the snows of her name, was helped into the sedan chair which would carry her to the temple of the Tutelary God. A great concourse of people lined the way and crowded about the temple to watch and listen.

The face of Snow Coral did not change. She did not even speak to Peach Blossom, although she had been granted permission to keep her faithful *amah* beside

254

her to the last. She looked straight ahead—and bowed her head as the ceremony was intoned in the dim light of the temple, doing homage to the huge wooden figure of the god in its gorgeous silken robes, which already stood at the end of the bridal table.

When all was over save the ceremony of the two candles, Snow Coral was to be left alone with her "husband." Again she asked that Peach Blossom remain beside her. Tong Shih seemed sad as she bade good-by to Snow Coral, because she wished the people to think she really sorrowed; but, departing, she slipped into the maiden's hands a knife of keen steel. And Snow Coral understood for what use that knife was intended.

She bade Peach Blossom sit in a far corner of the incense burdened room. Now that there were no other watchers there was no need of pretense, so she sat at the table of the candles. One candle, the dragon candle, burned before the god, a hideous figure, grotesque in its fantastic colorings. The second candle, the phœnix candle, burned before the drooping seated figure of Snow Coral.

"If only there were no people outside," said Peach Blossom, "we might open the door and flee."

"Wait!" said a voice that seemed to come out of the ceiling of the temple room, but that Peach Blossom knew for the voice of Ta Liu. "The time will come."

Her heart pounded with renewed hope. Perhaps the great stupid man had a plan after all.

The candles burned lower and lower. In a real marriage ceremony the first candle to extinguish itself indicated whether the bride or groom should precede the other in death. But now this whole ceremony was a farce, for Snow Coral knew she must die by the knife Tong Shih had given her.

Hours passed while the candles burned lower and lower. Fewer and fewer people could now be heard outside. Long after midnight it seemed that there was none at all—and it was then that the miracle transpired.

For the giant wooden god became a man! Ta Liu, the patient and crafty one, straightened from his long motionless vigil and smiled at Snow Coral and Peach Blossom to quiet their fears.

"Through the darkness behind the temple," he whispered, "three speedy horses await us, and warm clothing for us all!"

"Ta Liu!" gasped Snow Coral. "How did you manage to move away the god and take his place?"

"You still are big, as I said, but you are not stupid," cried Peach Blossom to the giant.

"It is well that I am big," said Ta Liu, "for none save a giant could have moved that wooden image, and worn its robes without exciting suspicion, and none save a skilled kitemaker, who is used to handling colors could have painted a mask so that it looked enough like the god's face even to deceive the people who worship. But come, for the way to Chefoo is long and there will be eager ones there to await us."

"Who will be there?" whispered Snow Coral, though already she knew.

"My master Kung Hao," said Ta Liu bowing, "and his father Governor Kung, and your father General Chu Ahead of us will go a fast messenger, bidding them all to be ready."

So the three slipped in secret from the temple of the Tutelary God and vanished into the darkness. With their horses was one lone man, tall and slender, the runner who was to precede them.

"Travel ahead," Ta Liu said softly to this man, "and find my master in Chefoo as I have already told you, and tell him that his bride is on her way to him, guarded safe from all harm by Ta Liu and the loyal—but rather stupid—Peach Blossom!"

The man moved away and Ta Liu strode after him for a space.

"As you go," he whispered so that Snow Coral and

Peach Blossom could not hear, "stop first at the house of Tong Shih. Tell her only this: that Snow Coral has disappeared from the temple and cannot be found. Tell her the evil she planned is known, and when she asks what she may do to avert disgrace, place this little gift in her hands!"

And Ta Liu, the giant, placed in the hands of his messenger the slender little blade he had taken gently from Snow Coral in the temple.

When spring came at last to sacred Tai Shan, and aged Tianfu under the mountain, two kites flew side by side from a garden where Confucius had dreamed in the long ago—two butterfly kites which soared and swooped in the laughing breeze.

THE END

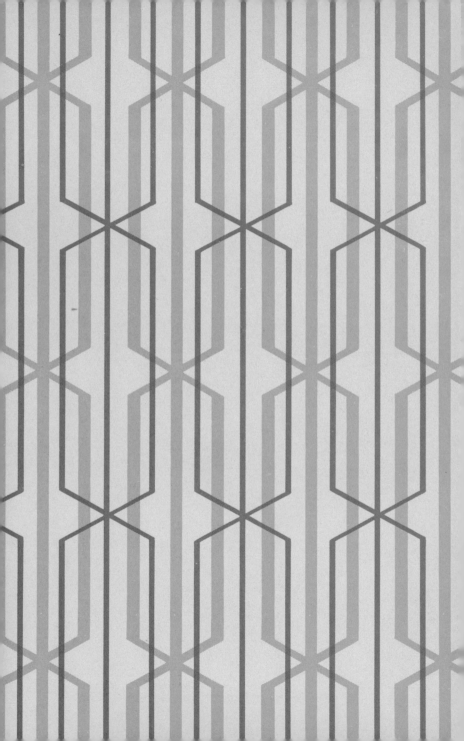